All
Those
Broken Angels

PETER ADAM SALOMON

All Those Broken Angels

flux
®
Woodbury, Minnesota

First Edition
First Printing, 2014

Book design by Bob Gaul
Cover design by Lisa Novak
Cover image by Lisa Novak

Flux, an imprint of Llewellyn Worldwide Ltd.

This is a work of fiction. Names, characters, places, and incidents are either the product of the author's imagination or are used fictitiously, and any resemblance to actual persons living or dead, business establishments, events, or locales is entirely coincidental. Cover model used for illustrative purposes only and may not endorse or represent the book's subject.

Library of Congress Cataloging-in-Publication Data
Salomon, Peter Adam.
 All those broken angels/Peter Adam Salomon.—First edition.
     pages cm
 Summary: Both haunted and inspired by the shadow of his best friend, Melanie, since her disappearance and presumed death when they were six, Richard, now sixteen, is completely unprepared when a new classmate, Melanie, arrives at Savannah Arts Academy High School claiming to be that same friend.
 ISBN 978-0-7387-4079-9
 [1. Missing children—Fiction. 2. Ghosts—Fiction. 3. Best friends—Fiction. 4. Friendship—Fiction. 5. Savannah (Ga.)—Fiction. 6. Mystery and detective stories.] I. Title.
 PZ7.S15415All 2014
 [Fic]—dc23
                                                          2014014104

Flux
Llewellyn Worldwide Ltd.
2143 Wooddale Drive
Woodbury, MN 55125-2989
www.fluxnow.com

Printed in the United States of America

To Andre Scara Bialolenki

ONE

On what would have been her tenth birthday, my best friend was declared legally dead. Only one witness was called to testify.

Me.

"I, Richard James Harrison, swear to tell the truth, the whole truth, and nothing but the truth. So help me God."

I'll never forgive myself for being the last person to see her alive. I just can't remember what I saw.

I remember what I had for breakfast: maple and brown sugar oatmeal. And orange juice. I remember what she was wearing: red shoes and blue jeans and a pale pink shirt she'd just spilled soda on. And a sparkling barrette in her long brown hair.

We were playing hide-and-seek in the bright Georgia sun. I counted to one hundred. I turned around.

I never found her.

We were six years old, together as always. I remember everything: a dog barking, the cars passing by, the smell of freshly cut grass. I counted to one hundred and then I turned around.

No one ever found her.

I tried to remember more, but every time I closed my eyes I would finish counting and I would turn around and she was gone. I closed my eyes and I was turning around and turning around and screaming her name. The dog barked. A car honked.

I counted to one hundred and turned around but I never found her.

And now, years later, I keep turning around, hoping to catch a glimpse of her. Only there's nothing but the dog and the car and the smell of freshly cut grass.

———

They questioned me about the last time I'd seen my best friend, about what happened on that terrible, lonely day. I placed my hand on the Bible. I swore to tell the truth. The whole truth. Nothing but the truth. So help me God.

But I lied.

The day after the Probate Court Judge declared Melanie Anne Robins dead, her parents buried a small box that held nothing but a dress. The one with polka dots she'd worn the first day of first grade. The matching socks, too. They told me they were moving away, but the words were meaningless. My parents told me they loved me, but the words were empty and hollow.

Nothing mattered anymore. No one understood.

Not at that miserable excuse for a funeral. Or the night after I counted to one hundred. After I turned around and never found her. That terrible, lonely night I first met the ghost of my best friend.

So help me God.

TWO

Hours after I turned around and screamed Melanie's name, after the dog barked and the car honked, my parents turned on my nightlight, kissed me good night, and closed the door. Sleep abandoned me, and the loneliness was a deep dark pit swallowing me whole. I was six years old and alone and lost and absolutely terrified.

And then Melanie walked into my room, into my life, into me. There was nothing to see, but I felt her, as though if I turned around quickly enough she'd be there, still waiting for me to reach one hundred. She was a shadow without a source, a presence I sensed but couldn't see. It had to be her; who else could it be?

I felt her, so close to me, and then the shadow cast by the nightlight shifted, breaking away from reality. It flowed across the floor toward my bed. I couldn't breathe, couldn't even blink as it reached for me.

I pulled the blanket higher to protect myself but my fingers were curled outside, and with one final surge the shadow cast itself over my skin.

It burned. The heat was the monster under the bed come to life, and as I curled up in the flames waiting to die, the shadow screamed inside my mind.

But through it all, through the burning and the bellowing and the heat and the fire and the flames, I felt Melanie's love for me and knew, without doubt, without question, without fear, one simple truth: my best friend was dead.

So help me God.

———

In the morning my sheets were drenched with sweat and my parents gave me medicine for the fever. Everything hurt, muscles and head and heart. They gave me more pills and goodnight kisses and let me sleep while search parties were formed, while strangers were brought in for questioning, while Amber Alerts were issued. The day after her disappearance was a nightmare that lingered long after I awoke. Melanie was gone, I was alone, and I couldn't remember anything.

Night fell like a dark cloak over the world and once again the shadow moved.

I was ready for it this time, sitting in bed, huddled within the sheets. When it came for me I scooted into the corner, drawing myself into a frightened little ball. I left none of my skin exposed; just two eyes peeking out.

The shadow reached above the sheets, searching for an

opening. Heat simmered off the darkness, radiating in waves. I was afraid to blink, afraid to move. My heart thundered in my ears and beneath the covers I grew hotter and hotter. The sheets were moist, sweat soaking through the fabric.

The top part of the shadow had dark tendrils spinning off like hair. The head tilted to the side as if studying me. Shoulders shrugged, and then it flowed far enough away for the heat to disappear.

A tendril pointed to the bed and drew an imaginary line between us. For a moment nothing happened; then it gradually crossed the line. Heat pushed me farther into the corner, and the shadow quickly retreated. Even with the distance, I felt the infinite, eternal sadness as it left me.

Two arms reached out and then she waved. Beneath the covers, I fought the urge to wave back.

My bedroom door opened and the light in the room shifted again, the shadow fleeing, leaving me alone, curled in the corner of my bed.

"How are you doing, sweetheart?" my mom asked, putting her hand on my forehead. "I think your fever's broken, at least."

"Fine," I said, but it wasn't true. Not then. Not now. The last time I was "fine" was that breakfast of maple and brown sugar oatmeal. I didn't know the words for what was happening to me, what had happened to Melanie, but there was a sadness growing within me, overwhelming and complete, filling the emptiness she'd left behind.

And I was so very desperate to fill that hole. Desperate enough to yearn for the simple act of a shadow waving.

Desperate enough to burn for the chance to hear her screaming inside of me again.

Desperate enough to accept her haunting me.

———————

My parents said good night and left me alone with the nightlight and the moon outside the window. I sat in the corner, watching the shadows for movement, and then threw off the covers. My pale skin shone in the moonlight, and I waved at the nightlight and the moon. In response, the shadow slid over the edge of the bed, approaching the imaginary line it had drawn.

I raised my hand, palm facing her. A gray arm rose, and where we touched, my skin tingled; the pain more bearable than the night before, the heat less. The shadow was quieter, almost subdued, and I felt the apology in the subtle welcoming warmth.

Most of all, I felt her. Melanie was there, inside me, and I was whole again.

THREE

I flipped open my notebook as though I were going to take notes, clicking my pencil until all of the lead poked out so I'd have something to do, putting it back together. The blank paper stared at me and I drew a small circle in the corner, then tiny rays coming out to create a sun. As art it wasn't great, but I wasn't going for art. I was going for "It looks like Richard is taking notes," and at that I figured I was doing pretty well.

When the sun was finished, I took a quick glance around the room. Caitlin was hunched over her desk, blonde hair shadowing the notebook she was scribbling in. Under no circumstances would those scribbles be related to the history lesson we were getting. I doodled, she wrote. Behind Caitlin, Max was practicing his best "I'm paying attention" look. It wasn't as good as his "That's a very good point" face, which he usually saved for direct questions from the teacher. As a character actor, he collected goofy faces the way other students memorized monologues. Next to Caitlin, Logan focused on the teacher without blinking. His fingers tapped out a song on his desk as he smiled his action hero smile beneath his action hero hair.

I sketched a tall tree with cracks in the bark running to the ground and thin branches stretching to the sky. Beneath, I added grass, but there was something missing. There was always something missing. So I added what I always did, to almost everything I'd ever drawn, the art that had earned my acceptance to Savannah Arts Academy high school. Next to the leafless tree, under a bright sun, I drew a broken tombstone. And reaching from the dirt of the grave, a skeletal hand rose, casting a vibrant, vicious, feminine shadow.

"Macabre," they called my paintings. And "creepy." Sometimes "disturbed" or "morbid." That was always my favorite. My attempts to capture the way the shadow crawled across the floor, the way it had come to me every night for the past ten years. All those times the shadow experimented, learning to control the heat it put out, to lessen the volume of the screams. My ears rang for hours after each visit until she learned that control. Now it was nothing more than a whisper, tender and gentle.

That skeletal hand reached for me, always reaching and, without thinking, I added her name to the tombstone. In the corner of the classroom, the shadows shifted. She was never far away, always close enough to burn, writhing and waiting until we were alone and she was able to sink into me and come home.

I erased her name, the smudge of it left behind until

I shaded the tombstone some more, covering the erasures with darkness. Even though I wasn't looking, I knew the shadow was waving.

Max shook his hair in my direction to get my attention, the rainbow of dyes swirling every which way. Trying to get me to laugh. He'd been doing that since we first met. Not that we were friends; more like acquaintances who talked in school, but that was the extent of it.

Caitlin glanced up as I was watching Max. She smiled through the fall of her hair, but I didn't smile back. I never did. She was worth smiling at, but I'd made the mistake of returning her smile once. That night, the shadow ignited. Hotter than hell, the flames swallowed me when I lifted the blanket to expose my skin. She wailed, deafening, and beneath the agony I felt her hate, her jealousy.

After that I knew there would be no more smiles.

I'd lived like this for ten years now. Every day and every night since Melanie had disappeared. Since we buried her dress. Since her parents moved away, unable to cope with the mystery and the depression. Melanie's shadow filled the hole inside of me, and I could live without smiles.

Caitlin shrugged, turning to her notebook and her poetry. Max made silly faces and Logan stared at the teacher and I drew. Just the same as every other day.

A knock sounded at the front of the class. The principal stuck her head in and nodded to Mrs. Pierce before opening the door wider and walking inside. A petite girl followed, long hair shadowing her face. She held a backpack in front of her like armor, as though protecting herself from our scrutiny.

"Class," Mrs. Pierce said, moving to stand closer to the girl and blocking the shimmers of copper sparkling in the shadows of her hair. "We have a new student joining us." She rested her hand on the girl's shoulder and steered her toward an empty desk in the front row. As they approached, the new girl looked around the room. For a moment our eyes met and for no reason at all I found myself smiling.

Mrs. Pierce pulled the chair out for her. "You can sit here, Melanie."

In the corner of the room the shadow screamed, burning the air around me until I couldn't breathe, couldn't move, couldn't think, and everything went black and everything changed and everything disappeared and all I knew was pain. Unending, unceasing pain.

FOUR

The linoleum was cool against my skin as I opened one blurry eye, my vision refusing to focus. Voices tumbled over each other around me and somewhere far away there was a distant smoldering ache, but, even as I focused on the floor, the heat disappeared. Everything hurt but nothing made sense. Someone close to me was saying something and it took far too long to realize it was my name.

"Richard?"

The room spun as I turned to Mrs. Pierce.

"Hey, Casper," Logan said. "You look as though you've seen a ghost."

Another student laughed and another said something I couldn't hear.

"Wake up," Logan said, kneeling to stare at me, his eyes unblinking. "Damn, you're alive." He smiled, but it was colder than the floor. "Where's the drama in that?"

Max tugged on Logan's shoulder, pulling him out of the way.

"Richard?" Mrs. Pierce said again. "The nurse is on her way. How are you feeling?"

I blinked her into focus. The room tilted a little, but other than that everything worked.

"Okay, I guess."

Around me, the other students pretended they weren't watching. The new girl wasn't visible from where I was and the shadow had fled, leaving a harsh emptiness behind.

The nurse escorted me to her office and took my vitals in the small examination room, but there was nothing to find. There never had been. The years of therapy my parents had demanded after I first told them about the shadow had failed to yield anything discernible to modern science. "Peduncular Hallucinosis" they called it. A fancy term for an imaginary friend replacing the best friend I'd lost all those years ago. "Perfectly normal response" to fill-in-the-blank: depression, stress, loss, and/or loneliness. "He'll outgrow it."

During the sessions, the shadow, never far from my side, would wave to me while the doctors taped various electrodes to my skin and ran their tests. There was nothing for them to find. It was all in my head, they told me. Imaginary friend, indeed.

"I called your parents to come pick you up," the nurse said, writing my perfect temperature in her notes.

"I'm fine," I said. "I'd just like to go to class."

"Fine?" She shook her head, an attempt at a comforting

smile crossing her face. "You passed out again. You know the procedure; we have to send you home."

"I need my books." Anything to get out of that small room, back to where the shadow was hiding. Back to a girl with Melanie's name. It lingered, that name, like the ringing in my ears after the shadow visited.

The phone rang and the nurse returned to her office to answer it. As soon as she left, I went the other way, out the second door into the hallway. My footsteps echoed in the empty hall as I hurried to my history class. When I arrived, I burst in and everyone turned to look at me like I'd lost my mind. There was a different teacher talking to different students and I had no idea what class the new girl might have after history.

I kept walking, and reached the performing arts wing before the shadow caught up. She curled around my legs but didn't sink inside of me. She burned, flares of fire stinging my skin.

From another hall, a piano ran through a scale and then there was silence. With the shadow tagging along, I peeked through the window. Mr. Reynolds, one of the music teachers, played and then nodded his head.

A sweet voice ran through the same scale, note following note, one octave and then higher. I craned my neck to see more of the room. Sunlight poured through the windows in the corner, bringing out the highlights of her hair as Melanie sang.

She sang higher, warming up. The shadow writhed, stretching out, covering my arms. I didn't want to stop watching, but the shadow left me no choice, boiling hotter and hotter until I had to move. To run away until I no longer heard Melanie's voice. Only then did the shadow let me go, drenched in sweat and panting in the empty hallway.

I collapsed against a row of lockers with a metallic bang and slid to the floor. The nurse and my parents found me there some time later. Once again, the nurse took my temperature and, once again, it was perfectly normal. Everything was perfectly normal.

"Richard?" my mother asked in her "maternal" voice. I'd first heard that voice the night Melanie disappeared and it showed up with depressing regularity every time she wanted to tell me something but feared how I'd react. The first time she discovered all my drawings, she'd used it. Worried I was suicidal or something.

"I'm fine," I said in my "I'm fine" voice, honed after years of practice when I realized telling anyone about the shadow simply caused more problems. Easier to lie. Always easier to lie.

At home, they called my doctor and my therapist and anyone else available to call, but there was nothing wrong with me. My parents, like the school nurse and everyone else, had gotten used to the "seizures," as the doctors called them. The random shrieks, the constant burning, the occasional fainting. Just another day in the life of me.

I turned the shower on as hot as it would go, steam

billowing until it filled the room. I shut my eyes and let the water run over my face, attempting to remember the way the sunlight played with the new Melanie's hair as she sang.

To remember how the sunlight played with *my* Melanie's hair, right before I counted to one hundred and turned around and never found her.

She was gone, replaced by the ghost of her, and now another girl named Melanie had come into my life and the shadow didn't like her.

I had made my choice long ago. The first and last time I smiled at Caitlin. That night, I chose the shadow. I always chose the shadow. I would always choose *my* Melanie.

I dried off and stood naked and exposed, closing my eyes and waiting for the subtle heat of her embrace. She'd learned such fine control through the years, tracing languid patterns on my skin, leaving warm trails behind. Soft, exquisite heat. So very delicate.

But not tonight. Tonight, she burned. Tonight, she screamed. Tonight, she seethed and raged and writhed as she sank into me.

And then my arm moved.

She moved *my* arm.

I fought for control but she was too strong, too insistent, too demanding.

Her fingers uncurled.

My fingers uncurled.

I burned.

My arm moved. My fingers moved. The heat flared hotter

until I surrendered. Her jealousy consumed me as my hand moved across the mirror.

I screamed.

Left behind in the steam were three words.

I

AM

MELANIE

FIVE

The alarm went off far too early. Sleep had teased me deep into the night as I waited for the shadow to come to bed, but she was nowhere to be found. Just the lonely corners of my room mocking me in the pale light of the moon.

The loss was a physical ache and it felt as though portions of me were missing again. I'd thrown the blankets to the floor, exposing myself to the cold lonely air, but when the alarm finally went off I was curled into a ball, shivering, the remnants of a dream fading. Everything ached, bone-deep and weary, and the act of sitting was far more difficult than it should have been.

I opened my eyes and only then noticed the mess surrounding me. Pieces of paper littered the floor like confetti. And on them all, scrawled in my handwriting, were the same three words that had been left on the mirror.

I
AM
MELANIE

I stared at the numerous paper cuts and smudges of ink the shadow had left behind on my hands. There was no memory to be found of the writing or the destruction. I remembered going to sleep and I remembered waking from a dream that left me shivering in my bed. Beyond that, there was nothing but a mess.

"Where are you?" I asked the empty room, but there was no response. I sucked the blood off the deepest paper cut and started throwing away the scraps of paper.

Situated in Ardsley Park, surrounded by the stately houses and parks that give the city its charm, Savannah Arts Academy was a three-story, square block of an institution that, from the outside, has little stateliness or charm. As a charter school struggling to keep the arts alive in public education, there was only so much they could do to make the building stately or charming. But thanks to its reputation, Savannah Arts drew the talented and creative from all over southeast Georgia, creating a thriving community of artistic teenagers studying everything from dance to drama, visual arts to music.

The cafeteria was standard issue, other than the artwork

lining the walls. Parts of theater sets masqueraded as art while actual art was used in posters to advertise performances and other events. Scattered around at random intervals were framed paintings by students and alumni.

On the far wall, close to where I always sat, a bulky frame held a watercolor I'd entered in a contest my freshman year: a grassy field, pale green, each blade seeming to move in an unseen wind. An equally soft carpet of wildflowers. The entire piece felt delicate, like a caress. Even the bony hand reaching through the flowers, grasping for something just out of reach of the drawing.

And, as always, a skeletal shadow trailed behind.

———————

"Is this seat taken?" Melanie asked, holding a brown paper lunch bag. The table was empty, and she walked around to slide into the chair across from me before I had a chance to answer. Her hair was tied up, exposing a long pale neck and almost elfin ears with small silver hoops dangling from them.

Sunlight filtered through the windows high above, glistening off her skin and casting a thin shadow on the table.

The heat singed as it burrowed into my flesh. Through the fire I felt the shadow's jealousy, her anger, and I found myself writing letters on the table and knew, without looking, what three words the shadow was forcing me to spell out.

"Why do they call you Casper?" Melanie asked before taking a bite of her sandwich.

Adrenaline flooded me, the urge to flee so strong my

feet had pushed me from the table before I had time to stop myself.

Melanie's eyebrows arched as I stood, but she merely took another bite of her sandwich. Despite the discomfort, the need to escape, I sat and clutched my legs to get them to stop moving.

"My name is Richard." The words came out clipped, through gritted teeth.

"I know," she said. "You don't remember me, do you?"

The shadow shrieked to wake the dead. I pressed my index finger to my wrist, counting each beat of my heart. I counted to ten, then twenty, deep breaths every five, praying just to endure the noise. Nothing worked, and by the time I reached one hundred all thought had melted in the heat.

"I'm Melanie," she said. "I remember you." And then she reached across the table and stretched out delicate, almost skeletal fingers and rested them on my arm.

With the contact, the shadow was gone. The silence complete. The air-conditioned air cool and simple on my flesh. Where the empty hole inside of me should have been, Melanie's touch grounded me, driving the darkness away and bringing so much light there were no shadows left.

Her eyes were a shade of blue darker than I believed possible, glistening with unshed tears.

After ten long, lonely years, I felt whole without the shadow inside me.

"In elementary school," I said, staring at the table to keep from watching her cry, "after my best friend died, I told everyone she was still there. That I still played with her.

Kids are cruel. They called me Casper for having a ghost for a friend. I guess I never outgrew the name."

For a long time she was silent, so long I wondered if she was even paying attention. When I looked at her, tears had drawn long trails on her cheeks, wetting her lips.

"I missed you," she said, the words so very soft. And then, even softer, "I'm so sorry, Richard. There's so much to tell you."

SIX

I was about to speak, to say something, anything. To deny her existence, to protest her pretense of being my friend, but the bell rang, flooding the room with noise. Melanie flinched at the sound and hastily wiped her tears away with a cough.

"I have to get to class," she said, before standing so quickly her chair fell to the floor with a loud metallic crash. She flinched once again and ran from the cafeteria before I even stood.

It was difficult to focus on any one image as the linoleum passed beneath my feet. I randomly bumped into classmates but didn't feel anything until I stopped in the middle of the hallway as people wandered by. I might have blinked. Maybe not. Just stared, without seeing, past hundreds of students. Seeing only into the past.

But, even now, there was nothing to see. I counted to one hundred. I turned around. She was gone.

The sounds of the school were muted, lost in the ringing in my ears as the shadow returned to me, bringing heat and comfort and friendship. Filling the vast holes in my broken, lonely soul, the overwhelming emptiness inside. She was there. She had always been there.

———————

After school, I sat in my Neon and said a little prayer to the "falling-apart car gods" that the old Dodge would crank. Sure, the car was unreliable and had a tendency to stall when going uphill, but I lived in Savannah and the only hills were highway on-ramps. I had long since learned to avoid I-95 and most of the time, if the car started once, it'd stay on until I got to wherever it was I was going. Could be worse, I guessed; I could have had to ride the school bus.

Instead of driving home, I headed to what passed as work.

The ghost industry in Savannah, like in New Orleans and other haunted cities, was part and parcel of the tourism industry. Growing up with a ghost, besides causing the inevitable bullying, had led me to make far too many research trips to the library and the Internet. As I attempted to understand my best friend, the shadow and I became experts on "Haunted Savannah." Each cemetery had its own legends and myths. Houses and businesses were filled with ancient beliefs and hauntings.

We visited every site, staying out long past curfew so we'd be there at the stroke of midnight, and woke early to catch the sunrise on the river. There were photographers around who specialized in electronic analysis of haunted houses; psychics and charlatans, mediums and faith healers. And none of them ever noticed a ghost waving at them. No one ever asked about the shadow at my side.

At age sixteen, the only jobs that interested me were with the many Savannah ghost tours. I wasn't a guide yet, just working the cash register at the kiosk on River Street, but I loved the atmosphere, the search for something more, the desire to experience the unexplained. Tourists were always hungry to believe, desperate for proof of something they wanted to be true.

I knew the tour would be light on a school night, unless I could drum up business on River Street. Plus, it was a beautiful evening, and if there was an open seat I was always invited to fill it at no charge.

And then Melanie walked by, alone on the cobblestones, watching the people and the river.

The shadow flared as I tried to wave. My muscles contracted with the heat, forcing the movement to stop. I closed my eyes to block out the sight of Melanie's hair catching the sun, but I wasn't sure if it was a voluntary act or not.

When I opened them she was nowhere to be seen, and the shadow slowly released me. I blinked, ridiculously happy to be able to control my own eyelids again.

It was really more of a glorified trolley than a bus, with hard wooden seats and big windows. By the time of the first tour of the night, it was only half-full of tourists, laughing as they took clichéd pictures of each other. The guide waved to me as I slid into an empty bench and rested my head against the seat, staring at the ceiling. He started his pre-tour patter as one last group of tourists arrived. They filled most of the remaining seats, and then one final person climbed up. Her hair caught the last fading rays of the setting sun, her skin shining with the brush of light against it, and, from everywhere at once, the shadow surrounded me.

Heat blossomed, pushing me against the bench, but if anyone else noticed anything other than a sudden, unusual warmth, they didn't show it. The shadow darkened, filling the seat, but there was nothing to be done as Melanie sat down.

"Is it always so hot on these things?" she asked, tying her hair into a ponytail.

I shook my head, struggling to speak as the shadow sank into me.

"No," I managed to say. "AC must not be working."

"Do you give tours, too?"

"No," I said, fighting the shadow to let me get that one word out.

"Do you like ghosts?" she asked with a smile. "Or is this more of that Casper thing?"

I shrugged and, deep within, tried not to burst into flame next to her.

Melanie touched me as the trolley pulled away from the curb and the tour began. Once again the shadow fled at the contact, leaving me in silent peace, the loneliness absolute.

"Just a job," I said.

Her smile faded as she studied the point of contact between us. "I'm sorry," she said, removing her hand. "I keep saying that, don't I?"

Beyond her the shadow waved and then slowly, oh so slowly, approached, stretching darkness out until I waved back. The shadow flowed over my flesh, sinking into me with a subtle warmth and a quiet sigh. Almost, but not quite, an apology.

"I had a friend named Melanie once." I stared out the window as the parks of Savannah rolled by. "She died."

The guide's narration continued on but I wasn't listening. There was nothing new to hear other than the quiet breathing of the girl sitting next to me.

"I remember playing hide-and-seek with you," she said. "I remember running through Forsyth Park and trying not to trip, laughing as you hopped to keep up."

I cleared my throat but wouldn't, couldn't, face her. "She died when we were six."

"No, Richard." She pulled at my arm to get me to turn to her but I didn't move. "There's so much to tell you. So much you never knew. So much I never knew. Please, look at me. Please?"

"That invisible friend?" I said, not focusing on anything beyond the shadow surrounding us. "It was my only friend after she died. It still is. I know you're new in town. I'm sure Logan or someone else wanted to screw with me. What else is new? I'm used to it by now. He knows 'Melanie' was her name. He must have thought this was too good to pass up."

Behind me, her breath caught on a sob and I closed my

eyes for no reason other than I no longer wanted to see the sunset caught in her hair. I no longer wanted to see anything at all. The shadow kept me warm, the shadow sang its wordless song inside my head, the shadow filled me as Melanie softly cried.

SEVEN

When Melanie spoke, her voice was rough, with none of the music I'd heard at school when she sang. Now it was full of tears and memories.

There was nowhere to go, nowhere to hide. Lost in the shadow's embrace, I had nothing to do but listen.

"Richard," she said, so very quietly. "There was a box in my room. Under my bed, remember?" Once more, she sobbed, speaking through the catch in her throat. "Please, Richard. Do you remember that?"

Without turning to her, I nodded. I remembered. A long, heavy box I wasn't allowed to play with. Almost a trunk, with a dented metal clasp. Her mother had yelled at me the one time I pulled it out from its hiding place. I never tried again. It was an insignificant memory I'd never shared. Not with anyone. Only Melanie could have possibly known.

The shadow exploded deep inside, and on the window

my finger wrote three very simple words against my conscious control.

"That day you turned around to count," Melanie said, her voice coming from a great distance, muffled and difficult to hear. "I felt so scared and alone. Hell, I don't know what I felt. So much still doesn't make sense. I just had to run. To run and keep running and never stop, can you understand that?"

When I didn't respond, she kept talking.

"I remember being cold. Shivering and freezing; running kept me warm. I ran until my feet bled through my shoes. Through trees and bushes, until I was all scratched up and I hurt and I just kept going. I couldn't stop. I ran all day, until I didn't think I could run any more. But even then I kept going. When the sun set, the need to flee just disappeared, like it had never been there at all. I was so tired. I collapsed, right where I was, in the middle of nowhere."

I turned around when she didn't continue. She was crying, hair shadowing her. Every so often her shoulders heaved. Around us, a couple of people glanced over and then quickly looked away as the tour continued through the heart of Haunted Savannah. Within me, the shadow was silent, distant, and very lonely.

"When I woke," Melanie said, "I could barely move, I hurt so much. I crawled through the woods, unable to stand. I must have crawled for hours until I came to a road and lay down. I was bleeding and scared and so miserable; you have no idea."

I considered reaching out to her the way she'd reached

out to me in the cafeteria, but the shadow flared before I even started to move, keeping my hands at my side.

"Melanie," I said, but she either didn't hear or didn't care.

"Finally, a car stopped. The woman had to carry me to get me inside. She gave me something to drink and then I must have fallen asleep on the drive to her house. She bandaged me and fed me and then I slept in her living room, with all these family photos on the wall watching me, protecting me. I was so tired, I never even told her my name. But it didn't matter. She'd seen the news, she knew who I was. So, while I was sleeping, she called my parents.

"See, Richard," Melanie said, her tear-stained voice coming to life as she turned to stare at me with red, bloodshot eyes. "I was going home, back to my family. Back to you."

"What happened?" I asked, the words barely spoken out loud.

"My mom answered," she said. "I guess everything would have been different if someone else had answered. My dad, or the police, anyone. I'd have come home and nothing ever would have changed. Instead, a few hours later, my uncle arrived. He thanked the woman and then took me to his house."

"My mom showed up late that night, once she was able to sneak out of the house without anyone noticing. It took years for me to piece all of this together, until I understood even this much." She shook her head, the motion causing stray strands of hair to stick to her tear-stained skin. "The box, Richard. Do you remember the box? Please, I need to know."

The shadow tightened its embrace but I fought through

the pain, through clenched teeth, and forced out the words. "I remember."

Melanie deflated next to me, as though all the air had escaped from her. A harsh, ragged cry, and then she was silent. Tears, heavy and constant, poured from her. For a long moment the only sounds were the PA system and the tour bus itself.

"It was for me," she whispered. "That box. If I was bad, or loud, or my father was angry."

The shadow burst into flame, screaming as if to wake the ghosts in the haunted houses we were driving by. Screamed and screamed until there was nowhere else for the screams to go but out of me. Every head on the trolley turned to stare, and I swallowed the half-escaped shout. I looked out the window, away from their prying eyes, and the tour continued with some nervous laughter and a joke from the guide.

My tears felt as though they were about to turn to steam. And then Melanie reached out to me and the shadow fled from her touch, leaving me in blessed, glorious peace.

"My mom told my uncle everything when she got to his house," Melanie said. "About my father locking me in the box. About the beatings, the bruises. Everything." She flinched, squeezing me. "He wanted to kill my dad. He wanted my mom to stay there and never go back home, but she loved my dad so much. She just wanted what was best for me, no matter what. Then she kissed me goodbye, and I never saw her again."

Melanie took a deep breath, letting it out in a long sigh. She rubbed her palms into her eyes and then turned to me.

"So much didn't make sense, then or now. I don't know what compelled me to run that day. Or why I couldn't stop." She attempted a smile, but it didn't last very long. "An old friend of my uncle's lives in Alabama. The middle of nowhere, raising his family as far off the grid as he can. Lots of home-schooled kids. They took me in, raised me. Hid me from my dad."

With the shadow gone, I covered her hand with mine, our fingers merging with a deep, primal need.

"A few months ago, my dad arrived on their doorstep. He told them he'd been searching for years. He'd brought the sheriff with him. They had no choice. He says he's changed." She shrugged. "So far, I believe him, I guess." Her voice trailed off into silence and she closed her eyes. She sniffled once, wiping her nose. When she finally spoke again, her voice was whisper soft. "He told me about my mom," she said and then opened her eyes. "That she died."

I swallowed what I'd been about to say: that I'd watched from across the cemetery as her father prayed in front of the two gravestones, Melanie's and her mother's. That no one else had attended the funeral. Not even the shadow; just her father and me.

"After we got to town," Melanie said, "I was going to go to your house, but he wouldn't let me out of his sight until I convinced him to let me go to school. I didn't know you'd be at Savannah Arts."

"You found me," I said, squeezing her even tighter.

She smiled, tentative at first, before squeezing back. Then she let go to brush loose strands of hair off her face. It didn't matter the reason, though. The moment she released me the shadow returned with a vengeance, searing straight through me until all memory of Melanie's touch had vanished.

Next to me, she kept talking, but the crying of the shadow drowned out her voice, drowned out the world. There was nothing but impossible noise, incredible heat, and indescribable hurt until there was nothing at all.

EIGHT

When I opened my eyes, Melanie was calling my name and the tour guide was shaking my shoulder with a very odd look in his eyes.

"Tour's almost finished, Richard," he said. "Think you can make it?"

I nodded, and he smiled before turning to the tourists, joking with them as he walked to the front of the trolley and started the tour again.

"Are you okay?" Melanie asked.

I took a deep breath, feeling the stiffness the shadow left behind. Ignoring the surreptitious stares of everyone on the tour bus, I kept my eyes glued to the view passing by outside the windows without seeing anything. There was nothing out there I hadn't already seen before, but I didn't have the strength to turn and face Melanie. Every so often I heard her crying, and if I closed my eyes I saw those precious tears coming to rest on too-pink lips shining in the flickering light of the trolley.

I squeezed my eyes tighter, blocking out the image, but it was too late. The shadow melted the memory to cinders, leaving nothing but darkness behind before subsiding to a dull roar within.

———————

The tour ground to a halt and I stumbled off the trolley to my car, pretending not to hear Melanie following behind. As I opened the door, she reached out and spun me around, sending the shadow deeper into hiding.

"Richard," she said. "Please, talk to me." There was an odd, hesitant quality to the words, almost pleading. Infinitely vulnerable.

To the west, the sun was slipping past the horizon, giving the city a soothing orange glow that matched what leaves remained on the trees. There was a chill in the air, or what passed for a chill in a Savannah autumn.

"Get in," I managed to say, forcing the words out. I stood there waiting to see what she would do, too large a part of me hoping she'd just walk away.

Instead, she stayed silent and headed around the car. The Neon cooperated and started the first time.

"Where are we going?" she asked, but the shadow kept me from answering. Melanie simply getting into the car felt like a victory.

She called her father as we drove, her voice quiet as she

told him she was studying at the library on Bull Street. I've no idea if he believed her. It didn't matter anyway.

We headed east, up President Street to Penn and then Bonaventure until we reached the cemetery. The setting sun cast long shadows on the black iron fences, the tombstones and statues, and the Spanish-moss-draped trees reaching out to the few people wandering the grounds this late in the day. There was something special, spectral, to the quality of the light that spoke to me with whispered cries and tremendous heat.

I headed toward the new section of the cemetery, far less visited than the gothic tourist sections. The shadows blanketing the cemetery captivated me, called to me, spoke to me, and the shadow within answered with cries of her own. There was an empathy there, a piercing compassion. This happened every time I visited, and I was always visiting with my sketchpad. So many drawings, it wasn't possible to remember them all.

Sometimes I'd be painting so intensely, with such focus, it no longer felt as though I was in control of the brush flying rapidly over the canvas. I'd finish and sign my name and wonder where the passion and inspiration had come from. But I never dwelled on it too much; sometimes, I thought, it was better not to question creativity lest it disappear and never be found again.

A light breeze set creeping twists of Spanish moss waving, causing shadows to writhe around us as we walked through the cemetery. Just after the sun set, I came to a stop in front of a far-too-small tombstone. In the darkness it was difficult to make out the words, so I took out my phone and shone the light on it.

Behind me, Melanie gasped. It was the only sound. The shadow burned with a terrible longing, burned with a vicious glee, burned with a tremendous ache, and inside me there was nothing but a desperate need the burning filled.

MELANIE ANNE ROBINS
BELOVED DAUGHTER

In the silence, I heard Melanie crying, but I was far too exhausted to turn to her. There was an all-consuming lethargy spreading through me, as though I were far older than sixteen. Closer to death than birth.

With the cool Savannah breeze blowing through the lonely trees, I swung the light from my phone to the larger tombstone next to Melanie's.

She dropped to her knees in the grass of her mother's grave.

"Mommy," she said, reaching those delicate fingers to the tombstone.

The pale light of the moon caught her motion, casting a frail shadow on the grave, and I realized I'd been drawing the scene in front of me for most of my life.

I turned around, unable to watch her grief. I let her cry, walking far enough to give her at least a semblance of privacy. I turned and opened myself to the shadow, aching for the heat to envelope me and take me away from the crying girl on her mother's grave. But the shadow was silent, the chill in the air raising goose bumps on my flesh as I stood all by myself in the middle of the darkened cemetery.

"Richard?" she called to me, and when I turned she was still on the ground, her fingers resting on her own tombstone. "I'm me. You believe that, right?"

I closed my eyes, picturing the six-year-old girl I'd grown up with. Remembering only her. Trying to forget about the ten years I'd spent with a ghost as my only friend. Ignoring the weight of all the graves surrounding me, the stories contained within them. The sad, sad tales each could tell if only someone like me would let them in.

"It's me," she said again, her voice pleading. She pushed against her own tombstone trying to stand, but her legs betrayed her and she collapsed to the ground.

The shadow was silent as I closed the distance between us, between a girl named Melanie I barely knew and a girl named Melanie I'd never forgotten. At the edge of her grave, I stopped, unable to close the gap any farther. Too much separated us—years and secrets and the ghost of my best friend.

I turned around and walked back to the car, quiet as she ran to catch me, silent as she talked to me, unable to hear her over the gentle whisper of the shadow kindled within.

NINE

Rather than take Melanie to her car, I drove us home. After ten years, I figured my parents deserved to know. Her quiet sobbing had subsided to an uncomfortable, melancholic silence, and we sat in my parked car for a moment, no sound save for the engine knocking itself to sleep.

"Thank you," she said with a sniffle. "For taking me there."

I shrugged, unable to think of a response beyond a limp "You're welcome," but there was nothing else to say so I said nothing at all.

"My dad mentioned something about going," she said, talking to the window more than me. "He never did. I guess he didn't want me to see my own grave."

When I didn't respond, she sniffled again and didn't say anything more until I got out of the car. I waited for her to walk the crumbling brick path with me and held the front door open for her. My parents were watching television in the living room and glanced up as I poked my head in.

Whatever they might have been about to say melted away when they saw I had company with me. Their lonely, solitary son who hadn't brought anyone home in well over a decade wasn't alone. If the night weren't so overwhelmingly depressing, I might have laughed at the shock on their faces. And I hadn't laughed in a very long time.

"Mom, Dad," I said, standing in front of them feeling as though I'd fallen down a rabbit hole. "This is Melanie."

The television rambled on, broadcasting random sitcoms to an ignored laugh track, but in my living room there was an overwhelming silence. The shadow circled me, refusing my embrace as it studied Melanie, and even without the contact I felt the jealousy, the accusation I'd brought *her* into our house.

"Hi Mr. Harrison, Mrs. Harrison," Melanie said as she made her way to the couch. She sat perched on the edge of the seat as though afraid to make an indentation on the fabric.

My parents were silent as Melanie stumbled through an abbreviated version of the story she'd told me on the tour bus. My father reached to my mom halfway through, but they didn't interrupt.

"Richard," Melanie said, turning to me as her story ran down, "it's really late. Can you drive me to my car? Please?"

My parents remained on the couch, silent as we walked out the door. We were almost to my car when my mother came running after us, my father right behind. She ran to Melanie, her arms stretched wide, and Melanie melted into her embrace.

Streaks of mascara stained my mother's face, and I flinched as my father rested his arm on my shoulders, the weight strangely reassuring in the chilly night air.

"Welcome home," my mother said, barely loud enough for me to hear from where my father and I were pretending to give them some space.

I opened the Neon's door for Melanie, waiting for her to disentangle herself. Then, again in silence, I drove her to the river, pulling next to her car and waiting until she drove away. I sat there far longer than I'd planned. Sat in an empty car in an empty parking lot, staring at nothing and wondering where the shadow was.

By the time I got home, my parents were waiting for me at the kitchen table.

"It can't be her," my father said, his voice gentle. "Can it?"

I stood there, withstanding their sympathetic scrutiny, and swallowed everything I'd thought to say while driving home. I swallowed the doubts, the questions, the agonies, the memories, and faced my parents' tears with none of my own.

"Does it matter?" I said, then turned around and walked to my room.

———

I locked myself in, turning on only one lamp to increase the presence of shadows, but I was alone.

"Where are you?" I asked, the words soft, encouraging. But there was no response.

I took out a blank canvas, tightly stretched on its wooden

frame, and placed it on my easel. Set out my paints and my brushes. And then I studied the blankness, brush in hand, trembling with the need to paint. With the desire to create. But there was nothing there. The brush shook, flinging small droplets of paint to the floor like blood, but I couldn't find any image within me yearning to be free.

With my eyes closed, the all-encompassing whiteness of the blank canvas took on a life of its own, growing until it was all I saw. It mocked me, that emptiness, taunting me with my inability to create.

A solitary tear wet my cheek, and, as I wiped it away, my arm cast a long shadow across the canvas.

The shadow boiled as it crawled over my skin, flowing to my fingertips until the brush steadied. The shadow cried as we filled the blank canvas with light and darkness that contained an intensity of passion far beyond what I had ever been capable of expressing without her.

I painted for hours. I painted until my hand cramped and then continued, reveling in the heat and the flames, drowning in the rhythm and melody of her desolate song. I painted long after the ache became unbearable, long after I could barely stand, until the painting was complete.

The rising sun sent vibrant, vicious, feminine shadows dancing around my room. On the canvas, the same little girl I'd always drawn, with long dark hair, skipped merrily among the thorny roses growing around a tombstone. She was smiling as she reached out of the painting, beckoning to me.

It took all my remaining strength to raise my arm, but I finally managed to rest my fingers on her outstretched palm, the paint just the slightest bit tacky to my touch as though she didn't ever want to let me go.

The shadow slid into my heart as I touched the painting. Only this time, in place of screams, a little girl's wicked laughter filled me with a bitter ache.

TEN

Despite how late it was, when Melanie turned onto her street it was lit bright as day. News vans lined the road, some of them parked on sidewalks and lawns, as strangers stared out their windows at the metal garden of antennas sprouting up. Spotlights illuminated the crush of reporters and cameramen surrounding her house. She slammed on the brakes before anyone even noticed she was there and ducked beneath the steering wheel.

Her breath caught as she bit on her lip and closed her eyes, fighting the tears. When she peeked above the wheel, they were still there, dozens of lenses facing her door. She watched her father pacing in the living room, his shadow moving against the curtains. Every so often he slid them to the side and peeked out, flashbulbs popping at the motion.

Melanie rubbed her palms over her face with a sigh. As slowly as possible, she backed up and turned onto the street she'd been on, and only then did she start shivering. Her fingers clutched the wheel, gripping so tightly it was impossible to drive, so she just allowed the car to coast to a stop in the middle of the road. Deep gasping breaths did nothing to stop the pounding of her heart or the feverish shakes that made her entire body shiver. Still, she kept breathing, her eyes closed as she put the car in park and sank into the seat.

Someone honked, startling her so much she slammed her head into the window. When she finally looked, there was someone behind her trying to get past, and she put the car in drive and pulled to the side of the road. The driver flipper her off as he passed, but she didn't have the energy to care.

Taking a deep breath, she turned the radio on, scanning the stations until she found one covering the news. Her own name was the first thing she heard. With her eyes closed, she leaned back in the seat to listen.

"Melanie Anne Robins, missing since 2004 and declared legally dead almost six years ago, has allegedly returned to Savannah." The newsreader's voice was chipper, reporting such good news. Every word seemed to echo with her smile even through the radio.

In the car, Melanie swallowed her tears, scrubbing her face with the bottom of her shirt before turning the radio off. She wasn't really sure how the news had gotten out, but she understood the appeal of her return to a 24/7 news cycle world. She just had no desire to walk through the crowds and have her every move filmed. For a brief moment, she considered returning to Richard's house, but it was far too late and she had to go home.

She put the car in drive and drove to her street, parking far down the block. In front of her house, the crowd hadn't moved. If anything, it had grown as more news organizations heard about what was going on in this small neighborhood in Savannah. It was going to take something even more interesting than the reappearance of a missing girl to get them off her lawn, and Melanie figured that wasn't going to happen any time soon. She'd have to deal with them eventually; just not tonight.

She fixed her makeup as much as possible in the visor mirror, wiping the fading remnants of tears away. Then she practiced a smile, pasting it on despite the sobs still threatening to burst out of her. Perhaps, in the flickering light, it looked more like a grimace, but it would have to do. She closed her eyes, took a deep breath, and then got out of the car, forcing her feet to make as little noise as possible as she slipped behind a nearby house. Like a thief, she scaled a couple of fences, scraping her arms on a rusty metal gate before finally making it to her own yard.

The back door was locked, so she had to knock, and when her father answered his shadow stretched out, covering her completely. The house was too small for even just the two of them, and nothing like the home she'd been raised in. There, the sounds of children were a constant presence. Here, the place was always too quiet, too sad, for laughter.

He blocked most of the light as he followed her into her small bedroom. At more than six feet and approaching three hundred pounds, he was closer to three times her size than two. Melanie smiled her over-practiced grimace of a smile and waited for him to yell at her.

His fingers clenched, but he didn't yell. She saw the anger just under the surface, had known the triggers her entire life, and recognized the signs even in the dim light. But he took two harsh, ragged breaths. Deep, filling out his shoulders until they seemed to touch each edge of the doorframe, those breaths enlarged him somehow.

"It's late," he said finally, his voice calm but tinged with something darker. "It's a school night."

"I know," Melanie said. "Had to do some homework. Was just easier at the library."

When the breath left his body, he seemed to shrink. He took a step toward her, his hand raised to check his watch, and she flinched without thinking.

"Smart," he said, "using the back door. They've been here for hours. Showed up right after I got home from work."

"Why?" she asked.

"You." He shrugged, and then attempted a smile that didn't work. "You've returned from the dead."

She closed her eyes, swallowing the urge to start shaking again. "Tell them to leave."

"I called 911 but they're on public property, not breaking the law. The police also want to speak with you, said they'd send someone. Nothing else we can do." He shook his head and then turned around. "How is he?" he asked after a long silence. "Richard, right?"

Melanie stumbled to the bed, sitting when the mattress pressed into her legs. "I don't know."

"It's been a long time, Melanie," he said. "People change. I'm sorry." For a while he stood there watching her cry, until finally he closed the door and left her alone.

She slid to the floor and pulled a battered guitar case from under the bed. Curling into the corner with the instrument, she strummed the few chords she knew and then softly began to sing.

The words were barely more than a whisper, sad and full of longing. It was all she remembered of the lullaby her mother had sung to her, all those nights inside the box.

Other than the song, there was no noise until her father's shuffling gait once again approached her bedroom. She stared at the knob, waiting for it to turn, for him to barge in, his anger finally unleashed, but the door remained closed.

She continued softly singing until she heard the snap of the lock slide home on the outside of her door.

ELEVEN

At school the next morning, news vans filled most of the parking lot, filming as we headed inside. A handful of students were surrounded by reporters, bright lights shining on them as they answered questions. As far as I was aware, none of them even knew Melanie.

It had been far too early when my parents woke me to show me what was on television. News reports had played through the night on all the local channels, broadcasting static images of the front of Melanie's house. One intrepid reporter had even included a photograph of her gravestone, most likely taken sometime after Melanie and I had left the cemetery. But no new information was given, nothing beyond her alleged return, which was still not officially acknowledged. If a crime had been committed, the police would get involved, but having listened to Melanie, I wasn't sure what that crime might be.

Only the ringing of the bell made the reporters leave the students alone. But they stayed outside, waiting for her to finally appear.

When I reached my History class, Logan was leaning on the desk next to Melanie, his long legs almost reaching her chair, blocking everyone passing by. He wore his leading man smile, but the vacant stare from his pale, brown eyes gave the lie to the good looks, as though he wasn't fully paying attention to anything other than his hair. He smirked at me as I made my way to my seat, and in ignoring him I also ended up ignoring Melanie.

Perhaps it was for the best. The shadow coalesced in the corner, tendrils spinning off and waving, a twisting mass of darkness and heat only I saw.

Caitlin bent over her notebook, lost in the fall of blonde hair. Max smiled, and then turned it into a broad frown as I failed to smile in return.

"One of these days," he said, twisting his face into a crooked grin, "you're going to succumb to my charm."

"You have no charm," Logan said, walking to his seat.

Max laughed. "Prince Charming, at your service, My Lady," he said, bowing to Caitlin, who wasn't paying any attention at all.

Melanie looked back once, but I didn't return her smile, though Logan did, running fingers through his all-American hair as he stared at her.

Max drummed on the desk, the rhythm carrying through the room on an undercurrent of song, and a number of students tapped their feet in time with him.

Caitlin scratched out an entire page of tightly written words, the sound of the pen adding a subtle counterpoint to the percussion as Mrs. Pierce rambled on.

Barely ten minutes into the class, the PA system came to life with a burst of static.

"The school is now in lockdown. This is not a drill. Please shelter in place."

Mrs. Pierce locked the door as the announcement boomed through the school again, far too loud, almost distorting the words. She took a deep breath before flipping the light switch, plunging the room into shadows.

From somewhere down the hall, someone screamed.

Again, the automated message repeated.

"The back of the room," Mrs. Pierce said, her voice breaking despite how calmly she'd locked the door. "Quick." She waved toward the opposite wall, as far from the door as possible.

No one moved for a long moment, and then we all stood at the same time, crashing into desks and each other as we hurried to huddle at the base of the wall.

"Quietly," she said, crawling beneath the window of the door until she reached the rest of us and counted every student.

I found myself sandwiched between Logan and Melanie. He pushed against me to get me to move, but there was nowhere to go.

At the front of the room, the shadow flowed past the window, pressing against the glass for the space of a heartbeat before rushing like a tidal wave across the room and slamming into me. She was a warm, comforting embrace full of safety and peace.

Melanie rested her fingers on my arm, and still the shadow remained warm and gentle. On the other side of me, Logan saw the contact and drilled his elbow into my stomach.

I doubled over but no one had seen his action, and Mrs. Pierce just told me to be quiet when I groaned in pain.

A number of students had their cellphones out, texting and calling friends and family. One student said something had happened at an elementary school nearby but no one knew what that something might be.

"You okay?" Melanie asked, her voice quiet.

I shrugged, afraid to make a sound as Mrs. Pierce glared at me.

"They lost a kid," a girl by the window said. "Not a shooting."

"There's a lockdown for that?" another student asked.

"There's a lockdown for everything," Max said. "The principal at my last school was having a bad hair day and we all had to be wanded to get in the building."

Again, Mrs. Pierce told us to be quiet, but as more cellphones came out the atmosphere changed, with scattered reports it wasn't a shooting.

"Third grader named Sue, I think," one of the girls said. "Anyone know anyone at Windsor Forest Elementary?"

Everyone shook their heads, and even Mrs. Pierce let out a sigh.

We sat there until the all clear sounded on the PA system, everyone spreading half-heard rumors about the missing girl.

The news was limited to jumbled second-hand accounts from other students around the district, and little made sense.

Outside, one after another, the news vans packed their equipment and raced out of the parking lot. The story of the return of a missing girl had been quickly replaced by the countywide school lockdown.

Mrs. Pierce walked to the front of the class, and when she flipped the switch, the light was blinding. The principal made an announcement on the loudspeaker directing everyone to the auditorium, where we'd wait for our parents to collect us. Even those of us who drove would have to be signed out by a parent.

"Where's the auditorium?" Melanie asked.

"Follow me," I said, and made my way through the slowly moving mass of students.

By the time we arrived, the place wasn't even half full, and it didn't seem like it was going to be an enjoyable wait. I kept going, leading Melanie down the hallway behind the auditorium to the stage entrance.

We sat backstage, hidden from the audience by the thick velour curtain.

"You act?" she asked.

I shook my head. "Paint," I said. "I'm here for visual arts, drawing and stuff. You?"

"Singing." She rolled her eyes with a quick smile. "They like to refer to me as 'technically proficient.'"

"That's good, right?"

"Well, I think it's what they say when you're a good singer but not a great singer."

"What's the difference?"

Her laughter held music within it, reminding me of the scale she'd sung at the piano. "Probably the same difference between a good painter and a great one."

I nodded. "I'm pretty sure I'm both."

"Both?"

"Sometimes I can't paint at all," I said, fighting to get the words out past the sudden flames of the shadow within.

"I can't sing," Melanie said. "Well, I can but it feels like there's always something missing. Karaoke, I like to call it. Just good enough, I guess."

"I'm sorry."

"I had a vocal coach once who decided I needed to experience more, whatever that means. Then he told me it was because I'm a virgin," she said with a bitter laugh. "You can guess what his solution was. Needless to say, I ended up with a new coach."

I tried to match her smile, tried to return her laughter, but the shadow drowned my amusement into silence.

Every few minutes, we heard names being called out as parents arrived to collect their children. I leaned forward and pushed the curtain to the side only far enough to take a quick look out. Next to me, Melanie moved closer so we could both see. Most of the students had already left, but the place was still loud.

"There's Max," Melanie said. It was pretty impossible to miss his colorful hair. Next to him, his father rested his hand on Max's shoulder.

"And Logan," I said, as he walked away, his mother

holding his hand and pulling him after her. He broke loose from her and then glanced over his shoulder as I quickly let the curtain fall into place, certain he'd seen us.

"How are you doing?" I asked as we stopped spying on everyone. "The news showed the circus outside your house last night."

She smiled, but it faded as quickly as it had appeared. "Okay, I guess," she said. "I'd rather they just leave me alone, though."

"Missing girl returns," I said. "It's a big story."

"I know. I just don't really want to be a story." She shook her head with a laugh. "My dad called the cops on them. Didn't help. I had to sneak out the back door this morning to get to school."

"They were already here."

"I noticed."

"They've left, though," I said. "Right after the lockdown."

"Not really the reason I wanted them to leave, you know?" Melanie sighed as she rested her fingers on my arm. "Are you always this warm?"

"That's what my mom asks," I said. "Then she takes my temperature and it's normal."

She turned to me, breaking the contact only long enough to brush her hand across my forehead. "Feels warm," she said.

The shadow ignited as I drowned in Melanie's dark blue eyes.

"Richard Harrison," came the call from the other side of the curtain, and the moment dissolved into memory.

"I have to go." My voice cracked on the words. I peeked

through the curtains. The auditorium was almost empty now; only a handful of students remaining in their seats.

"I know," she said, reaching her hand out to me but letting it fall short.

She followed until we entered the auditorium in the seating area, since I figured arriving from backstage might not be the best idea. They'd called my name a third time by the time we reached my mom.

"Melanie," my mom said, "where's your father?"

"He commutes," she said. "He works out near Metter, I think. Not sure how long it'll take for him to get here."

While my mom went to talk to the principal, Melanie smiled at me, but I didn't have much joy within to smile back. So many emotions had shriveled away to nothingness over the years.

I fought to smile, but the muscles wouldn't move, my teeth wouldn't unclench, and deep inside, where parts of me withered in the flames, the shadow's gentle whisper drowned out the memory of her eyes.

TWELVE

She struggled to open her eyes, the lids so heavy. Far too heavy. Heavy and weighted down with something damp, something that smelled overwhelmingly foul. Smelled of sweat and something spoiled and rotten and something else she couldn't name. Didn't want to name.

She struggled to remember her name. It was there, somewhere. Somewhere deep inside. But all the thoughts and all the names and all the words were floating, sliding as she reached for them in the darkness. There was nothing but those heavy lids and the dampness pressing on them and the darkness and the floating thoughts. Floating free.

She struggled to move, but nothing worked, nothing moved. A finger, just a finger. Twitch, please, just for a moment, an instant, anything, anywhere. But nothing moved. So heavy. Damp. She strained to open her eyes, to remember her name, to move, but there was nothing. Nowhere. Her tongue rested heavily against her teeth, tasting of metal and fabric. Every breath filled her lungs with stale air, old and overused.

A voice spoke somewhere in the darkness, somewhere in the depths of the shadows. It might have been a word, it might have been a name. The voice was soft and hard and far away and far too close and there was nothing but the word and the word was meaningless.

She struggled to open her eyes, the lids so very heavy. Strained to remember her name, but her name wasn't whatever word the voice might have called out and she couldn't respond and couldn't move and couldn't follow the random pathways her thoughts wandered as the heavy darkness pressed on her. Far too heavy.

And there was nothing to be done but pray to dream the nightmare away.

THIRTEEN

Only after a time-consuming call to Melanie's father did they allow my mother to sign her out, and we all drove our own cars to my house. The radio was filled with thinly sourced reports about the disappearance of a third grader in the middle of recess at Windsor Forest Elementary, but they still hadn't released a name.

As we entered my room, Melanie walked to the easel. The drawing of the little girl reaching out of the picture stared at us. "It's lovely. I thought you said you weren't a great painter."

I shrugged as she turned to study the artwork covering the walls and piled on my desk. Countless pictures of skeletal hands casting vibrant, vicious, feminine shadows. Countless graves and always the same little girl, smiling as she beckoned to me.

"Well, obviously *you're* not a virgin," she said with a wicked laugh before sitting at my desk.

The shadow surged and I knew I was blushing. I turned from Melanie, throwing myself on my bed and pretending to study a large drawing of a twisted tree that had long since lost all of its leaves. A broken skull peeked out from a crack in the bark. Bloody tears fell like sap from an empty eye socket.

"Sorry," she said, with that same musical laugh. "I'm out of practice at this whole being-friends thing."

"Me too," I said. "I haven't had any friends since you left."

"Why?" she asked.

When I stayed silent, she kept talking, staring at all the drawings watching us. Running her fingers lightly over the long brown hair swirling around the little girl in each painting. "She's beautiful," she said, stretching her fingers out to rest on the closest image. "Is she famous?"

"Famous?"

"She looks familiar," she said. "Like I should know her, somehow."

"Just a drawing," I said, turning to stare at the crooked grins of the little girls staring from the walls.

The shadow curled around me in our bed we'd shared for a decade. Her warmth was a safe, comfortable presence at my side, and I treasured the trails of heat teasing my exposed arms as she caressed me.

I stretched, and the bottom of my T-shirt rose just enough to expose a thin strip of skin above my belt. The shadow ran one solitary line of heat across my flesh, teasing warmth writhing against me with a sigh that was almost, but not quite, a moan.

"Richard," Melanie said, scooting the chair closer to the bed and reaching out to me.

The shadow cupped my face in her warm embrace and, for a moment that might have lasted an eternity, my lips were the only part of me on fire.

I turned to Melanie. "I was nine," I said, "the first time I told my parents about her."

"Her?"

"That invisible friend," I said. "I'd been at school and some of the other students were picking on me. I always ate alone." I ran my fingers through my hair, catching on some tangled knots and ripping them free. "I told them I did have a friend. You. You were my friend. I told them everything. That you were sitting at the lunch table, eating with me, keeping me company. That you were always there. Always with me."

I didn't have the courage to look at her any longer so I let my eyes close, let the shadow darken my vision until there was nothing to see, no loneliness to face alone.

"The school called my parents, suggested counseling." I stayed quiet far too long, letting the silence comfort me. "The day you disappeared? That night, you came back to me. Even now it feels like you never left."

The wheels on my desk chair squeaked but I kept my eyes closed. When the bed shifted as Melanie sat next to me, I still didn't glance at her. And then she rested those long, delicate, almost skeletal fingers on my face, trailing a different kind of warmth down my cheek. The shadow sighed, and the fire banked long enough for me to open my eyes.

"I didn't know," she said, so close her breath was a soft,

sweet kiss against my skin. She smelled of vanilla and cream and mint and everything I'd ever imagined she'd smell like and the deeper I breathed, the more of her I inhaled, until there was no place left inside of me for the shadow to dwell.

The sun blazed through the windows, casting away the shadows in the room, shining brightly on the bony hands reaching out of the artwork surrounding us. On my bed, Melanie smiled.

"I'm so sorry," she said.

I shook my head, reaching to cover her mouth. "No more, okay?" I asked. "Please. No more apologies."

Beneath my fingers, the softness of her skin was a dream come true as she leaned even closer.

But the shadow reached me first.

Writhing and seething and raging, the shadow exploded through my body, raking every inch of exposed skin. Echoes of the scream built on top of each other until it was impossible to tell when one scream ended and another began. I attempted to cover my ears with my hands, but my arms wouldn't move. Tried to let go of Melanie, but my fingers only tightened on her skin. I fought to blink, wanting to block out the surge of fear that drowned those beautiful eyes I'd been about to drown in.

My hands closed tighter, sliding down to rest on her long, pale neck, her pulse thundering under my thumb. Tighter, clenching to wipe the smile from her pale pink lips.

The shadow bellowed and burned and I watched from far, far away as Melanie fought for breath, fought to live.

I tried to rescue her, tried to relax the murderous grip on

her throat, but my fingers clenched tighter. With every frantic beat of my heart, Melanie's heartbeat slowed. Her hands stopped pushing against my chest. Her beautiful dark blue eyes closed.

And then the doorbell rang, and a moment later my mother knocked on my door.

"Melanie, your dad's here," she called out as she passed by on the way to answer the bell.

My fist jerked open and Melanie fell away from me. She took deep, gasping breaths, glaring at me as she cowered in the corner.

"Oh, God," I said, harsh and ragged, in control of my own voice once more. "I'm so sorry." But when I reached out to her she flinched back.

She crawled to where her purse sat half-under my desk. She kept her eyes on me while she pulled it out, knocking over my trash can with the motion. Hundreds of scraps of paper tumbled out, covering the floor.

She picked one up, glaring at me as she read my handwriting before bunching it into a ball and throwing it at me.

I didn't hear her leave. Didn't hear anything my mother said. Didn't hear, didn't care, didn't move, barely breathed, and begged and pleaded to die.

The shadow burned, but I was beyond burning. The shadow screamed, but I was beyond hearing. The shadow embraced and stroked and caressed, but I was beyond it all.

I buried my face under my pillow to block the sun and tried to fall asleep, only to wake hours later to discover the nightmare was real. I sat, but didn't have the energy to do anything more than stare at the mess on the floor.

Finally, my arm moved against my will, crawling along the bed to pick up the scrap of paper Melanie had thrown at me. I tried to close my eyes so I wouldn't have to look at it, but the shadow refused to let me.

I

AM

MELANIE

I stared at the three words, each letter scrawled in dark, malicious lines. My fingers burned until I turned the scrap of paper over, carefully flattening it out. When I was done, my other hand grabbed a pencil, holding it unsteadily in my fist, only the point sticking out as my hand moved across the paper.

GO

The pencil fell to the bed. I read the lonely word and then reached for the keys on my nightstand.

I had no idea where I was going, where I was being led, but anywhere had to be better than where I was, so I sneaked out the back door.

I pulled out of the driveway and my left hand twitched,

so I turned left. I kept following the shadow's directions until I'd made so many turns I had no idea where I was. I drove on, leaving Savannah behind as we headed into rural Georgia, south on 17 past Richmond Hill until, as the sun set, I reached Fort McAllister Road and crossed the Ogeechee River onto Savage Island.

The wooden bar blocking access to the campground was down and I had to get out of the car to lift it before parking in a small lot near some campers. With my phone to light the way, the shadow directed me through oaks dripping Spanish moss into the marshes surrounding the island. If there had ever been more than a deer track through the trees, it was gone by now. I kept going, deeper into the woods filling the state park I'd once visited on a school field trip.

My phone died, taking the makeshift flashlight with it, and by the light of the moon we continued on until, at the base of a towering oak, I came to a stop. I looked at the delicate tracery of bare branches stretching toward the sky, the majesty of the tree I'd been painting my entire life. The bark split as though bleeding sap.

I collapsed, dropping to my knees in the hard-packed earth. Or, perhaps, the shadow drove me to my knees. I clawed the dirt, tearing my fingernails in my frenzy to dig. Deeper and deeper into the cool Georgia soil until, after far too long, after slicing my hands on too many stones and roots to count, I stopped.

My fingers bled into the small hole I'd created at the base of the tree as the moon cast pale shadows around the far-too-small human skull staring at me.

FOURTEEN

I stumbled backward as the moon disappeared into the clouds, shadows swirling around me as the light faded. Heat pressed down from every direction, beating me into the soil, closer to the bones I imagined I heard calling from beneath the surface of the earth.

The skull stared, empty eye sockets watching my every move. The shadow approached with a fluid grace, almost a caress, delicately tracing patterns on the pale bone.

I tried to push myself to my feet, struggled to stand, but I didn't get very far before the shadow caught me, wrapping around my bare forearms with immense strength, far stronger than ever before. The shadow dragged me toward the skull, until I was close enough to reach out and touch it.

Fighting the mesmerizing pull, I fought against the tension tearing through me even as I reached out and grasped the skull in my hands.

I only had enough time to think how very tiny it was before the shadow exploded.

It was like embracing Hell, and I was gloriously damned. The shadow's cry ripped my soul into shreds until there was nothing left but a profane prayer damning me with each labored beat of my broken heart.

On my knees, I howled at the moon. I yelled until my voice was gone, and then I roared even more, aching with the need to give voice to the silent skull I held.

I cradled the fragile bone until the screams ran dry and the flames consumed me. The skull tumbled to the ground as I collapsed into the hole I'd dug, another bone stabbing into my cheek like a kiss.

In the soil, my finger pushed through the dirt, leaving one letter behind.

I

I counted to ten, and then kept counting, trying to still the frantic beating of my heart. Nothing worked as I pushed through the dirt, dislodging more bones.

AM

I tried to close my eyes, attempting to fight the pressure that forced me to stare at the skull sitting in the hole. It was so very small, such a precious little thing, so lost and alone out here in the wilderness, without a name, without someone to tell the tale of what terrible and horrible deed must have happened for this delicate skull to have been buried here.

MELANIE

For far too long I lay there, fighting to catch my breath, staring at the skull and trying to swallow enough saliva to soothe my ragged throat, struggling to survive the onslaught of the shadow. At last I pushed myself up, my legs rubbery as I stood in the middle of the small clearing. The hole from where the skull watched me was deeper than I remembered, and contained an assortment of small bones I hadn't noticed before.

I should take the skull, deliver it to the police with a map to where I'd found it. As I took a step forward, the shadow shifted, sending flashes of darkness through me, leaving no doubt in my mind.

There would be no police. Not now. Maybe not ever. Finally, the shadow settled, curling around the bones.

I sank to my knees to refill the hole, placing the skull reverently at the bottom. I studied the tree while I filled the grave: the cracks in the bark I'd drawn so many times, the thin branches swaying in the windy autumn night. I patted down the leaves and mulch in the hole and stood on shivering legs.

Trying to follow the trail to the car, I walked in circles for close to an hour before the harsh lights of the parking lot flickered through the trees. I sank into the seat with a grateful smile that only disappeared when the Neon refused to start.

I laughed then, there in the middle of a deserted parking lot in the middle of a deserted night. More than I'd laughed in years. Perhaps more than I'd ever laughed. A manic, just slightly deranged laugh ripping my throat to shreds and bringing fresh tears to my eyes.

Again I turned the key, and on the fourth attempt it started with a cough before sputtering out.

On the next attempt, it stayed on, and I plugged the phone into the charger and waited to see how many messages I had and just how late it was. Slightly after midnight, and all the calls were from my parents. Nothing from Melanie, who would most likely never speak to me again.

The laughter shriveled and died, leaving me hollowed out and empty inside. The shadow trailed a delicate caress across my skin until she covered my lips with a subtle kiss. My eyes closed of their own accord and I drowned in the memory of those dark blue eyes, so near and yet so very far away. The kiss continued, the heat surging through me with a passion I'd never known as the shadow entered my mouth, entered me, with a quiet, gentle whisper.

FIFTEEN

By the time I got home, my father was asleep on the couch in the living room. My mom sat at the kitchen table, a cup of coffee in front of her. She looked at her phone, checking the time, before turning to me. "Almost one," she said, her weary voice just a distant echo through the ringing in my ears.

When I answered her, the soreness in my throat brought tears to my eyes, and even after downing a large glass of water it was difficult to speak. "Sorry," I said.

Her eyes opened at the harshness of my voice and she rested her palm on my forehead. "You okay?" she asked.

I nodded, since talking would hurt too much.

"Melanie?"

"Just hiking," I said. "Went down to Fort McAllister."

"Find what you were looking for?"

With a shrug, I turned away, taking another glass of water with me as I headed to my room.

"Richard?"

I stopped and glanced at her over my shoulder. She was standing in the hallway, leaning against the wall wearing her worried face.

"I don't know what I'm looking for," I said, "but I'll let you know if I find it."

In my room, I set out another blank canvas, but no matter how long I stared at it, there was nothing within to paint. Even though the shadow was a quiet, gentle presence, I felt more alone than I had in years.

Instead of trying to create, I gave up, cleaning unused paintbrushes and double-checking the seals on tubes and jars of paint. When I was done, it was two in the morning, but I was too afraid to sleep. To close my eyes and picture the fear in Melanie's eyes when my hands had wrapped around her neck or, almost worse, picture the empty sockets of the tiny skull staring at me. The fear of what my dreams would turn into was so frightening there was no way I was about to try to sleep.

I turned to my computer, playing online until I was so achingly bored that dreams sounded pretty good. Then I opened Google and rested my hands on the keys.

"Melanie," I said, the word scratching my throat. "I know you're here. I know you can hear me."

But the shadow was silent.

It had been ten years since she'd first visited me, ten years of my life spent with her always at my side. Ten years since that day when I turned around and counted to one hundred and everything changed. For ten years she'd been my only friend, experiencing everything life had to offer together, from elementary school to puberty to Savannah Arts Academy. We'd survived, we'd grown, and now she seemed to be hiding when I needed her most.

I closed my eyes, reaching to her the way she'd always reached to me. The lonely nights she'd been my constant companion and the terrible days growing up alone even though her shadow was never far away.

On the keys, my fingers twitched, and I typed what the heat led me to type, and only then did I hit Enter and open my eyes.

Dublin 1997

More than one hundred and fifty million hits, ranging from Trinity College, Dublin, to Dublin, Ohio, to a number of actresses I'd never heard of.

My finger burned, hunting and pecking the keyboard once again.

Dublin 1997 I am Melanie

There, almost lost amid the millions of hits, dozens from the *Courier-Herald* newspaper in Dublin, Georgia, appeared. Reports of a seven-year-old girl who had gone missing from an aftercare program at the local Methodist Church the year before I was born. Despite a massive manhunt and a number of wild goose chases, Melanie Elizabeth Bellemeade was never seen again.

The cries of the shadow were nothing but a gentle counterpoint to the harshness of my own breathing as I read about the short life of a little girl who had gone missing years before. There were a number of small black-and-white pictures, and in every single one she was smiling an all-too-familiar gap-toothed grin.

I turned to the artwork on my walls. The hair was different in my drawings—darker, more like the Melanie I'd lost when I was six—but the smile was all Melanie Elizabeth.

The shadow was a tender caress, wrapping around me as I said her name out loud, and only when she kissed me did I stop talking.

———

A long time later, as the sun crossed the horizon and the shadows in my room shifted with the fresh light, I printed out the articles about Melanie Elizabeth and hung them on my wall.

"Your mother would want to know," I said, my voice ragged from misuse.

The shadow twirled around me, pressing against my exposed flesh with a quiet embrace.

"The police, too," I said. "They can tell your parents where you're buried."

The shadow kissed me, lighting my lips on fire until my alarm clock went off and she fled into the recesses of my room.

"Does that mean I can call the police?" I asked before heading into the bathroom. As always, I turned the shower as hot as it would go, and when I got out the shadow seared my fingers until a single word was written on the mirror.

NO

SIXTEEN

At lunch, I was all set to sit at my lonely table and eat by myself, just like I'd done for pretty much my entire life, but as I crossed the crowded cafeteria, I saw Melanie sitting alone. I veered to the left, approaching her from the other side. The blue polo she was wearing matched her eyes and was buttoned to the top, covering most of her neck. A hint of a bruise poked out above the collar, and I tripped on an empty chair when I caught sight of it.

Melanie saw me and then turned around, taking a bite of her sandwich as she studied the crowd around us. I stood there, watching her chew. The bruises were darker up close, despite the coating of makeup she'd used to hide them. They were like a pair of matching hickeys, one on either side of her neck, about the size of my fingers and thumb.

"I'm sorry," I said, forcing the words out. If she heard me, she gave no sign.

The shadow stirred within, but Melanie paid no attention to me, continuing to eat her sandwich in silence.

I was about to leave when Logan appeared, pushing me aside to reach the chair across from her. "Is Casper bugging you?" he asked, sliding the seat back to knock against my legs, sending me even farther from the table.

Melanie smiled at him, bright and painful. "Not really," she said. "I'm ignoring him."

Logan looked over his shoulder at me before turning to her. "What a great idea," he said. "I should have thought of that a long time ago."

She laughed, a light, sparkling sound that drove the shadow into a rage. Or maybe the rage was all mine.

"Melanie," Logan said, leaning forward so he was able to reach his hands out and rest them next to her fingers. "What a beautiful name." She might have glanced at me for a moment, but she didn't move away from him. "I heard that you sing. I'm thinking of cutting out on lunch to practice. Interested?"

I ran from the cafeteria before I could hear her answer, stumbling against the chairs and tables in my way, pushing people aside, hoping to disappear, to melt into the shadows and be forgotten like the bones in the forest.

The shadow was quiet and calm as I ran, and I kept going until I reached the other side of the building. I had no place to go, outside or inside. I rested my hand on the emergency exit bar, thinking I'd go to the tree and visit those lonely bones, and I was about to leave when Max reached me.

"Well," he said, pulling my hand off the bar. "That would suck."

"What?"

"Setting off the alarm." He tugged until we were a few feet from the door. "It locks down the school, calls the police, etc. And with the whole Windsor Forest thing going on, not the best idea. So," he said, "what happened?"

"With?"

"Well, since I doubt you have any helpful information on the missing third grader, let's go with what happened with you and the new girl?"

I looked at him, at his smile, and the shadow was quiescent and compliant as I smiled back.

His eyes opened wide and he stumbled with mock surprise. "You're smiling," he said. "You never smile."

"I used to," I said. "You never knew me in kindergarten, before Melanie disappeared."

"No, but Logan filled me in when I first started here. Told me your name was Casper."

"It's an old joke."

"I'm not sure he knows the definition of the word 'joke,'" Max said before taking a deep breath, his bright smile slowly fading. "You mean she really is the same girl?"

"Same girl," I said.

"Well, imagine that, the news got something right for once," Max said. "They love reunion stories. Long lost girl returns home, big celebration."

"All those reporters lost interest the moment Sue Chapman went missing, I guess," I said. "Plus, I don't think Melanie's father wanted to make a big deal out of it. Neither did Melanie."

"It *is* a big deal. Ancient history now, but still pretty big. So, what happened?" he asked.

I looked out the window at the whole world outside waiting for me. "Everything," I said. "Nothing."

"Long story?"

I attempted to smile again but it was no use; the ability was gone as quickly as it had appeared. With a nod, I turned around and walked down the hallway. I heard Max behind me, but he soon went his own way. I kept going, past the cafeteria until I reached the rehearsal rooms, drawn by the faint sounds of singing, searching for something to soothe the beast within.

Logan sat at the piano, Melanie on the bench next to him. He played as they sang, their voices mixing and merging and floating through the air. Once he dipped his shoulder to press against her, causing her to look up and smile. Through the glass of the door, she saw me and quickly turned away. Logan followed her movement and stared at me. With a long, drawn-out smile, he also turned away.

I ran out the front door so the alarm wouldn't go off, racing through the parking lot to my car. The Neon started the first time, even blessing me with a little bit of air conditioning as I drove out of Savannah, down 17, to the small campground at Fort McAllister on Savage Island. Max called while I was driving, but I let voicemail answer it. There was nothing to say, no real need to listen to him vainly attempt to cheer me up when I felt anything but cheerful.

In the sunlight the entire area seemed different, calmer, safer. Bright sunlight shone on Redbird Creek as I wandered through the woods, the shadow leading me directly to the large oak tree. The clearing was so peaceful during the day, the sounds of nature calling out as I sat in the leaf cover, dropping my backpack next to me.

Nothing seemed to have been disturbed, and there was no real reason to unearth the skull again. The shadow filled me with respectful harmony as the sun cast shimmering shadows around the clearing, congregating about the gravesite.

My eyes closed of their own accord and, in the middle of a clearing on a quiet island off the coast of Georgia, surrounded by the bones of a long-dead little girl, I prayed.

I prayed to every god I'd ever thought to believe in. I prayed in silence and, when nothing happened, I prayed out loud. A heartfelt prayer full of every emotion I'd ever known. I prayed for myself, for the Melanie I'd lost, for the shadow I'd found. I prayed until the tears ran dry. And then prayed some more.

Through it all, the shadow rested a warm, comforting touch upon me, her wordless whisper a steady presence as she added her own prayers to mine.

I reached for my backpack and pulled my sketchpad out, leaning against the tree as I found a pencil. The shadow blanketed me until heat blossomed against my lips, and, together, we drew.

The outline came first: the shadings of a small, delicate figure, her back to me. Her head was cocked, staring behind her, out of the drawing, with large eyes so frightened and scared. The lines of the pencil bled onto the page, adding depth to the swirl of her hair, curls flying off in every direction. Subtle differences in the shading made it seem as though she were running, the hair bouncing with each step.

In the background, a large tree towered above her, throwing shadows out far enough to almost reach her feet. There, within the darkness, a blank and crooked tombstone sank into the earth.

My hand cramped and I took a deep breath, stretching out and studying the drawing. Her horror was palpable, a living, breathing thing, terror oozing slowly out of the picture, reaching for me.

Then I rested the point of the pencil on the outer edge of the page, the place where her eyes were staring in fear.

A single broad stroke left a hard, thick line across the paper. Then another, almost parallel. A harsh crescent of graphite connected the lines. The little girl's frightened eyes watched me draw. Two more harsh crescents almost touching her shoulder.

The pencil flew over the paper as I drew the rest of his arm, reaching for her, almost close enough to grab hold. Definitely close enough to reach her hair, to pull her closer, to press her into the earth at the base of the tree where her tombstone was sinking into her grave.

The shadow smoldered within as the little girl's frightened eyes stared in terror at the hand about to bury her, and for the first time I realized something I'd never allowed myself to consider.

Melanie Elizabeth Bellemeade had seen her killer. And she remembered.

SEVENTEEN

Melanie turned from where Richard watched through the door, turned to study the wavy soundproofing foam lining the walls, turned so she wouldn't have to see his face when she turned. Instead, she sang just that much louder, just that much faster, pressing Logan to keep up with her as the song ran in leaps and bounds around the room.

When the music ended, she closed her eyes, listening to the final echoes of the notes lingering in the air. Once more, Logan pressed against her shoulder, a heavy presence far too close, and she swallowed the shiver than ran through her. The bruises on her neck had been a faint, distant ache as she'd sung, forcing the words through her abused throat. An almost constant reminder of that moment when she'd been so close to losing herself in Richard's eyes, only to see them shift. The change was so subtle she wasn't sure she'd seen it at all as he disappeared inside himself, as his fingers tightened around her neck, as she struggled for breath.

The shiver came anyway, shaking her against Logan as he ran his hands over the piano keys, not playing music so much as just playing. Like the music was a game and he was winning.

She opened her eyes and turned to him, only to find him just inches away, as though he'd been studying her while her eyes were closed. She jerked back, almost falling off the bench before Logan grabbed her arms and pulled her closer, his grip just a little bit too tight.

"Careful," he said, "you could hurt yourself." He smiled, almost, but not quite, a sneer, and only after she matched his smile did he release her.

"Thanks," she said, sliding a little farther down the piano bench.

He let her go, merely continuing to smile as he played. "Again?"

He sang, the words resting lightly on the notes from the piano. As good a singer as he was, he was a better piano player, and it showed. Softly, she joined him, losing herself in the song to keep from thinking any of the thoughts that insisted upon being thought.

"No," he said, and again, "no." He pressed on the keys, interrupting the song. He turned to her, his smile just a memory. "Mr. Reynolds would probably refuse to teach you if he heard you sing like that. 'From here,' he'd say." Logan pressed his palm against her shirt, just below her ribs. "'Not from here.' Well, maybe he wouldn't actually touch you, but, really, all the fun is in touching you." His fingers came to rest between her breasts.

The pressure was hard against her skin, pushing the clasp of her bra deeper into her flesh. His thumb rested beneath her right breast and his little finger across her left. He smiled, pressing harder into her.

"From the diaphragm," he said, leaving his hand where it was. "You should know this by now, right?"

Melanie breathed in and nodded.

"I teach ten-year-olds who know that much," Logan said. "From here." He slid his hand to her stomach. "Not here." And, again, between her breasts, then farther, to her neck. He pushed the top of her collar down far enough to expose the bruises, and she flinched from his touch. "Doesn't help that you're hurt."

"I'm okay."

He reached out to let his fingers linger on her neck, fitting them to the bruises with a smile. "Whoever did this has smaller hands than me," he said. "Don't let any of the teachers see. They'll have to report it." His touch moved to her arms, sliding over her skin until he'd drawn her even closer to him.

"Again," he said when only inches separated them. "Stand up and sing for real this time. No more playing around."

She stood and the first note crawled out of her; the rapid beat of her heart disrupted her breathing and the pacing was all wrong. She sang, staring at Logan as he moved to stand in front of her. At the chorus, he traced the curve of her cheek with one hand as the other came to rest between her breasts, rising and falling with each breath.

"Stop, just stop—you're killing Mr. Reynolds and he isn't even here now," he said, interrupting her midway through. "Sure, the notes are on, but didn't anyone ever teach you more than the mechanics of singing? It's like something's broken inside of you."

"I know," she said, dropping her head to stare at his hand. It was a heavy weight against her shirt, and it took far too much energy to breathe.

Logan moved his hand far enough to rest the palm on her breast, and only then did she push him away. But that was all she did. It was all she'd ever done, meekly crawling into the box each and every night, never fighting back. Never striking out or making any sound at all.

"Isn't there any passion in you?" Logan asked.

Melanie sank to the bench and played with the keys, not pressing them hard enough to make any noise.

"Kind of a waste, don't you think?" He joined her, pulling her closer to rest his lips on her ear as he whispered. "All that heat, hiding inside you. Untouched. Just waiting to burn."

Again, she pushed him away, but he was far too strong and there was little fight left inside of her. Whatever fight might have been there had disappeared when he'd exposed the bruises. Faded with the memory of Richard holding her life in his hands. Now all that remained was a little girl, left to fall asleep in a small box beneath her bed while listening to a half-remembered lullaby.

Logan's lips were chapped against hers, harsh and hard and unforgiving, but her eyes finally closed and she returned his kiss. He tasted of soda and stale chips from the vending machine; nothing at all like what she'd always imagined her first kiss would be.

His grip around her tightened, and she blinked as his tongue entered her mouth. The fluorescent bulb hanging from the ceiling flickered once, sending crazy shadows pinwheeling around the room, and for a moment, an instant, an eternity, those shadows reached for her with a cry drowned out by the pounding of her heart.

When he let go, the shadows disappeared into whatever hallucination had created them. "Are you free next Friday night?" he said, the words accompanied by tiny kisses against her skin.

She shrugged against him, looking up long enough to catch the smile that was almost a sneer cross his face.

He kissed her neck, brushing his lips over the bruises before turning around and walking out of the room as the class bell sounded.

Melanie rested her head on the keys as the vision of Richard's fingers wrapping around her throat mixed with the image of Logan's kiss on her neck. Her breath caught on the memory of the click of the lock twisting home on the box. A dull, heavy thud echoing beneath the bed.

Small holes let in stale air and hazy light. She curled into a ball, making herself as small as possible, pressing her cheek against a hole. The stained carpet was the only thing visible as she listened to her mother sing somewhere far away. She remembered Logan's kiss and how close she'd been to dying in Richard's arms. She remembered the beatings and the bruises and, most of all, how much she'd always wanted to fight back, to stand up for herself. Instead, she'd always simply waited to be let out, waited to be saved, waited and hoped, most of all, to finally escape. To forget. To die.

EIGHTEEN

*She struggled to open her eyes, the lids so very heavy. The damp-
ness was gone, the weight lessened even though the darkness was so
very complete. Her breath sounded harsh and weak and rough in
her ears and when she blinked her eyes open, there was nothing to
see. Her head sagged from side to side as though it were separated
from her body and she had no control over it at all. The motion
came from far away, far removed and belonging to someone else,
and whoever it belonged to seemed to be laughing at her.*

*Her eyes blinked open. Her head slumped once more against
the floor and she saw the hard metal bars beneath her, support-
ing her. As her eyes adjusted to the darkness, the shadows moved,
twitching in the gloom. She fought to speak, but her tongue just
sat in her mouth, unresponsive, feeling like dead weight and tasting faintly sour.*

*She watched the shadows beneath her, through the bars she
rested on, battling to see, hair falling in front of her eyes. The*

shadows had a life of their own, writhing underneath her, but it was so difficult to think, to understand what she was looking at. Her thoughts ran in circles as she struggled to move and struggled to speak.

Her eyes closed and she fought to open them, pushing against the weight pressing her down, compressing her and making it difficult to breathe. She tried to make sense of the shadows twitching beneath her but nothing had made sense for such a very long time now. She attempted to remember her name, but there was nothing there to remember.

Her head sagged once more as she blinked and, after far too long, as her eyes failed, the shadows shifted one final time. There was a noise far away and far too close, a noise that might have been a word or might have been a sigh or might have been a moan but made no sense to her.

All that made sense was the single, eternal moment when the shadow beneath her, on the other side of the bars, blinked and opened its own eyes and stared at her, trying, it seemed, to speak or move, and failing.

All that made sense, as her head flopped to the other side once again, was when yet another shadow next to her blinked as well and, in the depths of the darkness, she was just able to see all of the bodies surrounding her, watching her, trapped with her, in their own cages, blinking and fighting through a haze of drugs.

They struggled to move, struggled to speak, struggled, most of all, to call for help. But the silence, like the darkness, was a heavy weight pressing on them, and when the voice came once more it came from far away, calling each and every one of them the very same name.

But it was not their name, had never been their name, and as they battled against the stench and the weight and the unrelenting pressure of the drugs, they fought to remember what their names had once been. But there was nothing there. Nothing but a shadow, blinking at them through eyes consumed by fear.

NINETEEN

A light rain fell on Savannah as I drove to work, the kind of brief, late-afternoon shower that served to clean the air and leave behind a glorious sunset. The streets glistened, reflections of streetlights and headlights combining with historic homes and towering oaks to create something slightly magical as I pulled into the parking lot near River Street.

Even with the rain and the slight chill in the air, the tourists were out and about, huddling under umbrellas. They waited for covered horse-drawn carriages and assorted trolleys, thanks to a number of local restaurants offering deals on dinner and a tour.

There was just enough room on the ghost tour for me to squeeze in toward the back. I always found something therapeutic about watching my city slide by in the rain, listening to the steady patter against the roof while the guide told tales of Haunted Savannah. In the fading light,

Colonial Park Cemetery contained a multitude of shadows and shades and ghosts, reaching out to me, and I found myself waving as we stopped to let the tourists take pictures and wander around for a few minutes.

I didn't have an umbrella, so I just let the water pour over me, plastering hair to my skin as I walked the familiar pathways, reading the familiar tombstones, reaching out to the wet marble of familiar statuary. The shadow kept me warm, boiling deep within, as I wandered, keeping away from the tourists until it was time to shuffle onto the trolley to continue the tour.

We'd just turned onto Broughton Street, behind a horse-drawn carriage taking a couple on a romantic after-dinner ride in the gentle rain, when the first faint echoes of police sirens cut through the storm.

Out the window, the flashing blue and red lights reached the trolley, sirens wailing as first one and then another police car sped by, splashing water on the carriage ahead of us. The trailing police car pulled into a half-spin, blocking Broughton a hundred yards ahead. After the tour bus pulled to a stop, tourists popped out of their seats, clamoring for a better view of whatever was happening. More police cars came from the other side of Broughton, and then even more from Drayton, until the entire area was a mass of flashing lights in the rain.

For a time, no one spoke. Everyone focused on the activity outside, but there was little to see. The guide clicked on the PA system. "Well," he said, somehow managing to find a cheerful tone, "it appears this tour might take a little longer than usual. No charge."

A few people laughed, but it was a nervous laugh with little real humor in it. Around me, tourists took out cell phones to check the news, but if anyone found anything, they didn't share it.

"We happen to be parked in front of the Marshall House," the guide continued, "which isn't part of the official tour but does have a history that might be of interest." He looked at me and waved me forward. "Best of all, we have somewhat of an expert on it here on the bus. Richard?"

Everyone turned to me as I made my way forward. Sure, I'd played around with the PA system when no one was on the trolley, even pretending I was leading my own tour, but this was a first.

"Hi," I said with an awkward wave, before the guide pointed at the button on the microphone that needed to be pressed. Which I knew. With a shake of my head, I hoped I wasn't blushing. Then I pressed the button.

"Hi, I'm Richard," I said, "and I guess I'll be your guide for a while." I smiled and the shadow smiled with me as I pointed. "On your left out there is the Marshall House, the oldest hotel in Savannah. It was once used as a Union hospital for wounded soldiers after the town was occupied during the Civil War. A lot of those soldiers died there. Young soldiers.

"In 2008, during the latest restoration, a number of odd events reported by the construction workers had slowed down the work. Missing equipment, and tools turning on when no one was near them, that kind of thing. So, this being Savannah, they called in ghost hunters. One of those was a photographer who told me what happened the first night they all stayed in the hotel."

Every eye was on me, even the guide behind the steering wheel. The rain was a soothing rhythm around us, creating harmony with my story. "Yes, they spent the night in what they believed was a haunted hotel. They walked through the building and tried just talking to the ghosts of Union soldiers dead almost 150 years, telling them they meant no harm. By the time the sun rose, they were all convinced that whatever energies might be hanging around the Marshall House were friendly. Just kids, about my age. It's said those scared, lonely soldiers are still hanging around, hiding in the quiet areas of the Marshall House, watching the lives they never got to live."

They clapped then. Even the guide. I waved and returned to my seat, shaking the offered hands of tourists eager to thank me for talking to them as we waited.

I had barely sat down when a tourist held his phone up. "They're saying someone called in about finding a body. They blocked off a couple of streets. Looks like it was just an animal, though."

After that, it didn't take very long for the police cars to drive off, leaving us to continue our tour as the rain stopped. Despite the interruption, everyone was in a good mood, tourists talking to strangers the entire time while the guide told his routine jokes.

By the time I got home, my hair and clothes were almost dry. I opened a local website to read the news about the false alarm. Turned out to be a stray dog that had been run over, which was depressing enough, but a tip had come in saying it might be human—might be a little girl.

I read through the latest articles on Sue Chapman, then read the old reports about Melanie Elizabeth Bellemeade. Another little girl who had gone missing without a trace. I opened SavannahNow, the website for the *Savannah Morning News*, and searched their archives for articles about Melanie in 1997. Not even a brief mention. The disappearance was apparently just a local story centered in Dublin, Georgia.

I was about to turn the computer off when my index finger began to burn, typing her name again and again into the search box, one letter at a time.

Finally, I rested my other hand on the typing finger until it came to a stop. "Melanie," I said, "the police need to know. They can find whoever did this to you."

But the shadow dissipated, melting away in the bright light of the monitor until there was no one in the room but me. Through blurry eyes, I read the home page of SavannahNow, scanning through the article on Sue Chapman and the desperate search going on in Windsor Forest. I also found one small article about the return of Melanie Robins to Savannah, but there was nothing to it, just a blurb reporting that no charges were pending in her mysterious disappearance.

When I was done, I deleted the string of Melanies in the search box and replaced it with *1997 Missing Girl* to see if that would bring something up. Over one hundred stories, but SavannahNow also wanted to know if I'd like to search the entire web and not just the *Savannah Morning News*. With nothing else to do, I clicked "Yes."

I scrolled through some of the three million hits without really seeing them. Name after name, country after country, state after state, city after city, a roll call of murder and kidnapping and rape around the world for a single year. Only then did the tears come.

So many names. So many stories.

So many shadows.

I clicked on some of the articles from Dublin about Melanie Elizabeth Bellemeade. Unfortunately, most of them were archived and not available online. I read one, an old interview with Jessica Bellemeade, a local veterinarian desperate to find her daughter. Her heartbreak was obvious—wondering where her child was, just wanting, needing, some semblance of peace, some form of closure.

"Melanie," I said, barely speaking out loud. "Your mother is still waiting for you." My voice broke on the words, coming out as little more than a sob. "Please."

But the shadow was silent and I was all alone with my tears.

TWENTY

By the next morning the rain had, in fact, cleaned the city, leaving Savannah to shine like a diamond at sunrise. The air held a last lingering breath of summer, a hint of warmth making a final visit. The shadow was nowhere to be seen, and a quick Internet search gave me the address of Melanie's new house.

The Neon was on its best behavior as I drove through the city. I took the most time-consuming route, delaying the inevitable as long as possible. Twice, I drove around Forsyth Park, remembering the days spent chasing after Melanie in the shade of the fountain. Now, college students played Frisbee and couples held hands as dogs tested the limits of their leashes. The park was crowded, even this early in the day, with tourists snapping obligatory pictures and children racing for the playground. On my second circuit, I gave up with a sigh. There was nothing more to do but get it over with.

When I finally arrived, a couple of kids were playing with rainbow chalk on the sidewalk while their mother was weeding next to them. A man wearing dark socks with sandals was cutting his lawn, but Melanie's house was silent.

I slowly walked to the door, still convincing myself not to turn around and drive somewhere, anywhere, else. A thousand apologies ran through my mind, the words stumbling into each other. I bit my lip, forcing one foot in front of the other, knowing, if nothing else, that I at least owed her this much.

The sound of the bell echoed, but there was no response. I rang again; still nothing. I was halfway turned around to leave when the door opened.

Melanie stood there and didn't say a thing, just stared at me, stared through me.

"Hi," I said, attempting a smile that didn't feel as though it came across as I intended.

She stayed silent, standing in the doorway, long strands of hair curling around her neck and resting on the fading bruises.

I looked away, looked at the ground, looked anywhere but at the marks I'd left on her, anywhere but at her unwelcoming eyes and her unsmiling lips.

"I'm sorry," I said, with as much sincerity as I could manage. "You said there was so much I didn't know, right?" The words just kept pouring out of me, anything to keep her from slamming the door. "Well, there's so much you don't know, Melanie."

When she shook her head, hair swirled around her face,

covering the bruises. "You can't be here," she said. "My dad's running errands and he'll be home any time now. Just go."

"Come to the river with me, then," I said. "Just to talk."

She closed her eyes and turned from me. "I always felt safe at your house," she said. "*Safe*. Do you know what that meant to me? Do you?" Her eyes, when she opened them, were red and harsh, and I took a step back from the force of them as the door slammed shut.

All the strength drained out of me with the echo of that slamming door. All the words I wanted to say slipped loose and hid in the shadows. In the window next to the door, delicate, almost skeletal fingers pushed the curtains out of the way. Melanie's dark blue eyes stared out at me. They glistened with tears, and then she was gone. Once more I was alone; an empty shell, fragile and raw and broken.

I considered just going home, but there was nothing for me there, nothing for me anywhere. The walk to my car seemed to take forever, and, once I got there, I did nothing but rest my head on the steering wheel. Finally, with nowhere else to go, nowhere else to be, I headed to the river to sit on a bench and watch the water flow by, as I'd wanted to do with Melanie. To tell her about the shadow. About the bones. About everything. About the other Melanie in my life. About Melanie Elizabeth Bellemeade and the mysterious man I think killed her. There was so much to tell, but no one was listening.

I watched the tourists taking pictures of the river, the boats on the water, and the colorful balloons kids were leading on colorful leashes. A musician played in front of an appreciative audience, filling the street with music, applause, and laughter. But the shadows stayed shadows, following the laws of nature rather than whatever laws Melanie Elizabeth had always broken to come to me every day.

"Where are you?" I asked, but the shadow was nowhere to be found.

"Talking to yourself?"

I turned around and saw Melanie walking out of the crowd. Even though she wasn't smiling, at least she was there. As she approached, the sun caught the highlights in her hair and cast a long feminine shadow behind her. Only as she sat on the bench did the shadow break free to curl like smoke around me, winding around my legs like a lonely cat.

"You're here," I said, but I wasn't sure which Melanie I was talking to.

She nodded. "I don't know why. My dad came home, and being here seemed the better place to be." She stared at the boats on the river. "He's drinking again. That was the biggest thing, when he said he'd changed. He told me he'd been sober for a while, looking for me. Now, lately? I don't know." A soft breeze carried long strands of her hair toward me, tickling my skin. "At least I'm too big for the box." Her laugh was a pale imitation of joy and did little to dispel the gloom. "Now he just locks me in my room."

"I—"

"No," she said. "I don't want to hear 'I'm sorry' one more damn time. Never again, okay? You changed, Richard. Right in front of me. You disappeared. One minute I think 'he's finally going to kiss me' and then, just as quickly, 'he's going to kill me.' So which is it?" Her voice, usually so soft and warm, was hard and cold. Quiet and loud, it drilled into my ears like the cries of the shadow. "Or is it just me? Is there something about me, something wrong with me, that says 'I'm a victim, hurt me'? Is that it?"

All of the apologies melted away, the words I'd practiced. There was nothing and everything to say, but I'd forgotten how to think and how to speak. How to open my mouth and produce sounds. The river sparkled in the sunlight, the entire city so alive and vibrant. Tourists wandered by, children laughing and playing in the warm morning sun.

"Melanie," I said, her name hanging in the air, the taste of it on my lips as a cloud floated in front of the sun and covered me in shadow. Her eyes shone with unshed tears, and, even now, surrounded by people, a hint of fear hid there.

"There's nothing wrong with you," I said, reaching out to her despite the shadow holding me back. Before I touched her, though, she slid down the bench until she was out of reach. I let my hand drop to the seat, picking at the green paint flaking off the metal. Again, I wanted to apologize, but I didn't think I ever deserved forgiveness.

Instead, I raised my arm, casting a long thin shadow on the ground. "They used to hook me up to this machine, to measure my brain waves. To see if I was sane, I think. They never told me if I passed or not." I moved my arm, making the shadow dance on the pavement in front of us. "A couple of years ago, I was so tired." I closed my eyes, blocking out the world. "Everything was impossible, I guess. I had one friend, and no one believed me. No one understood. No one cared."

I took a deep breath and then opened my eyes. The shadow curled around me, running warm trails over my arms in a desolate attempt at a hug. "I figured, if she couldn't be with me, maybe I could be with her. You were the only thing in my life worth living for, and you were dead."

"No," Melanie whispered. "Please, no."

"She wouldn't let me," I said, my voice just as soft. "She refused to let me die."

Next to me, Melanie was quiet.

"I couldn't stop screaming, but I couldn't move." The shadow curled even tighter around me, warm and comforting and safe. "My parents found me crying on the floor of my room. Ever since then, they've tried to understand. They don't," I said. "They can't, but they try."

"Understand what?"

"Everything. Passing out, or random outbursts; the doctors don't really have a name for it. My parents stopped questioning me and I stopped talking about an invisible friend, about the ghost of you." I raised my hand until it cast a shadow on her face. The stripe of darkness ran across her skin, one eye brighter in the sun and the other shaded and hidden away. One half of her lips shone and the other half was muted. "Your shadow," I said, and then let my hand drop to my side.

Deep within, where parts of me had always felt as though they were missing, the shadow burned and cried, and I burned and cried with her.

"She's here, now," I said. "Inside me. Next to you. Everywhere."

Melanie slid just a little farther away, until she was at the end of the bench, and then she looked all around us.

"You don't see her, do you?" I asked, and her eyes jerked open wide. "I always thought the ghost was you. You were gone; she was there. What else would I think? I was six years old and all alone. Can you understand that? And now you're here," I said, as a sailboat caught the wind on the river.

For a long while I did nothing but stare at the boats floating by, listen to the laughter of children as they danced to the happy sounds of street musicians.

"You're not a victim," I said. "And there's never been anything wrong with you. Why would you ask that? What happened?"

"Nothing," she said. And then, "everything."

"Everything?"

"You, Logan, my dad. Everything. Nothing," she said. "It doesn't matter. Or maybe it does; I don't know."

I spun around on the bench, sliding closer and casting my own shadow on her. "Logan?" I asked, his name numb on my lips as I pictured them singing together.

"Nothing I can't handle," she said, waving the thought away. "Nothing happened. I'm still a virgin, still just a decent singer." She laughed, hard and brittle. "See, I can even make jokes about it."

I laughed with her, but, if anything, my laugh was even more fragile than hers.

"If she's not me," Melanie asked after the laughter died, "who is she?"

I took a deep breath, then reached out toward her. When

she didn't move, I rested my fingers as gently as possible on her arm. The shadow flowed through me until it focused on the point of contact between us. "Warm?" I asked, and smiled when she nodded.

"You said you always are," she said.

"She burns me. And she screams, inside my head. That's what all those medical tests were for." I shut my eyes, unable to watch her watching me.

"Richard." She said my name so softly, I opened my eyes just to see her lips move.

"I think her name is Melanie, too," I said. "Melanie Elizabeth Bellemeade. She disappeared from Dublin, Georgia, back in 1997."

Melanie's breath caught on whatever she was about to say. Her hand went to her neck, to where the bruises had almost but not quite faded. "She hates me," she said, "doesn't she?"

"I don't know," I said. "There's so much I don't know. Lately, she's been testing her limits, seeing what she can do."

"Since I came home?"

I nodded. "I don't think she hates you. I think she's jealous."

"Of me?" Melanie asked, turning to me. "She's spent the last ten years with you. If anything, I'm jealous of her."

The clouds broke apart, letting the sun beat down around us. Embers of copper sparkled in her hair like flames, but nothing on River Street, nothing on the water, none of the people walking by were casting shadows at all. I waved, but nothing waved back.

"Do you see that?" I asked, looking at Melanie. But she had her eyes closed, a tear or two slipping free.

Within, the shadow was nowhere to be found. No burning, no screaming. Just an infinite, sacred silence.

"See what?" she asked, still with her eyes closed.

"Nothing," I said. "Nothing at all."

TWENTY-ONE

If anyone else noticed the lack of shadows on River Street in Savannah, no one said anything. All those strangers walking by, enjoying the bright sunlight, blissfully unaware.

"I spent my whole childhood trying to convince everyone you were here," I said. "Other kids made fun of me. For a while they called me Nearly Headless Nick, thanks to *Harry Potter*. The doctors tried all sorts of medications, and when I stopped talking about you, they said the pills must have worked." I smiled even though Melanie wasn't looking at me, even though I was still unused to smiling. "For so long, I dreamed of being able to prove to everyone the shadow was real."

"I've always liked the Ghost of Christmas Future," she said.

"Me too." I laughed, a quick burst of sound that did little to brighten the mood but was something, at least. "Know the funny part?"

"There's a funny part?"

"Now that I can prove it, I'm afraid to."

She turned to me. Long strands of hair twirled and twisted around her in the wind, shimmering in the sunlight. "Prove what?"

I took a deep breath, swallowing a thousand things I wanted to tell her. "Do you trust me?" I asked. "Despite everything, do you?"

Melanie shook her head. Melanie nodded. Melanie didn't move at all, just stared into me with those dark blue eyes. "No," she said, little more than a whisper. And then, "I don't know, Richard. Maybe?"

I was about to say "I'm sorry" one more time, but she kept talking.

"I want to," she said. "There's still so much we don't know about each other, so much time we lost." Her lips, shiny and pink and glorious, curled into just the hint of a smile. "Yes," she said finally, the smile lingering. "I've missed you for so long. I've wanted nothing more than to be here in Savannah with you."

"It's a little bit of a drive," I said.

"What is?"

"Proof I'm not crazy."

By the time I pulled into the parking lot on Savage Island, I was no longer sure this was the best idea. I was no longer sure Melanie trusted me; she was leaning against the car door, as far away from me as possible.

"Good place to dump a body," she said, attempting to make a joke of it, but the tension was obvious in her voice.

"More than you know," I said, not laughing at all as I grabbed my backpack out of the rear seat and led the way through the woods. The sun was warm and bright, and I wasn't sure I'd ever have the courage to do this at night again.

"This is proof?" she asked as we wandered in circles.

It had been easier to find my way with the shadow tagging along, but we were alone and I was a little lost. It took a while before some of the trees looked familiar and I found the small path leading to the clearing. The giant oak tree didn't cast any shadow at all.

"It's beautiful," Melanie said, spinning around to take it all in at once.

"It's a lot of things," I said. "I guess beautiful is one of them."

I sat, cushioned by the heavy layer of leaves scattered on the ground, as Melanie explored the clearing. She rested her fingers on the bark of the tree as she leaned against it, watching me, and when the breeze crossed the island, it agitated the branches and set countless shadows to dancing around us.

Melanie glanced at me at the same time the shadows flowed through the clearing. The shadow, sweet as honey, melted into me.

"She's here," Melanie said, looking all around, "isn't she?"

I pulled my sketchbook out of my backpack and touched

the point of my pencil to the blank page. "She's here," I said. "And I think she saw her killer."

"What?"

I stared at the shadows surrounding us. "Please, Melanie," I whispered, "show me."

The darkness stretched out, clinging to my fingers as the pencil flew across the page. A large hand reached out of the picture as I drew his arm and then his shoulders and, finally, his face. Thin and narrow, and ultimately empty. The eyes were bare sockets, nothing more than holes where eyes should be. No nose at all above thin smiling lips, exposing teeth far too sharp to be human.

"Richard," Melanie said, calling my name as I shivered over the sketchbook. "Are you okay?"

"Did you see the shadow move?" I asked.

"No," she said, her voice small and distant. "But I've seen them. With Logan."

"What?"

"He asked me out."

The shadow fled, leaving me numb and alone as I crawled to the other side of the clearing, scattering the leaves until I reached the base of the tree.

"When he kissed me," Melanie said, "the shadows moved. I thought I was imagining things."

I turned, unable to look at her, unable to face the reality of that kiss, and scooped piles of dirt out of the way with my bare hands until I reached the bones.

"The shadow led me here," I said. The skull fit into my palm as I pulled it out. "I think this is Melanie."

She yelled, the sound echoing through the clearing, and fell backward, scrambling away. Her eyes were frightened, opened wide the way they'd been when my hands were wrapped around her throat and the only thought I'd had through my fear was how soft her skin had been as the shadow attempted to kill her.

For a long time she was quiet, staring at the skull in my hands. Then she shivered and turned from me. She turned around and turned around and never looked back, running down the path toward the car.

After filling the hole in, clutching the skull in my arms, I hurried to catch her. Melanie was waiting at the car, and we drove home in silence. The skull was wrapped in a shirt in my backpack. I promised her a promise I wasn't sure I'd be able to keep—that I'd go to the police, that I'd tell them everything. But I wasn't sure what "everything" was; wasn't sure how to explain how I found a skull in the middle of an island south of Savannah without them locking me in a claustrophobic room with white padded walls.

Melanie didn't speak at all after extracting that one promise. Instead, she stared out the window, her head swinging, studying every shadow for flickers of movement, jumping at every sound, flinching every time I tried to talk to her until I dropped her off at the river.

The thought of Logan kissing her kept echoing through me, but it was just a pale echo of the shadow's jealousy. I counted to one hundred, sitting there in my car. I counted to one hundred and turned around and watched the boats on the river. I counted to one hundred and pulled the backpack into the front seat, buckling her skull in safe and sound as the shadow and I drove home. She curled around me, lighting my lips on fire with every kiss, leaving the memory of Logan to disappear in the ashes.

TWENTY-TWO

Melanie slammed the door shut and drove the deadbolt home, locking out Richard and the shadows and that skull. With a harsh breath, she ran through the small house until she reached her own room, slamming that door as well. She turned on every light, taking off the shade from the floor lamp to banish the shadows. The brightness hurt her eyes, but, as she curled into the corner of her bed staring at nothing, she almost felt safe.

It didn't last.

The door jerked open, bouncing off the wall. Her father stood there, half-in and half-out of her room. Even from where she sat, she smelled the harsh alcoholic haze of his breath. For a long moment, he just stood there, watching her. Then he took a step inside her room, moving in front of the floor lamp, casting his shadow over her bed. Over her.

She flinched, moving away from the shadow he cast.

He stopped walking and seemed to sway on his feet, causing his shadow to slide across her sheets, closer to her, and she drew her knees in tight to her chest, trying to hide.

"You look just like her," he said, only some of the words slurred. Each syllable launched waves of alcohol-laced breath through the room. "So beautiful." He wiped his eyes and then collapsed to the ground, landing roughly on his knees, sending his shadow swirling around her.

Melanie let go of the breath she'd been holding and relaxed her legs just enough to get more comfortable, still staring at the shadow her father cast on the floor.

He rested both of his hands on the edge of her mattress, his weight shifting the surface beneath her, and then slid the rest of the way to the floor. He leaned back with a weak sigh, studying her with blood-shot eyes.

"I never gave up on you," he said. "I don't think you ever knew I was married before I met your mother. She was a little older than me, with a baby. I thought I was happy. Everything changed when her daughter died. *She* changed. Then, after the divorce, I was so lost. Until your mother found me. She showed me what happiness really was, the day you were born. She gave me a daughter of my own. I never believed you were dead. I just couldn't go through that again." He wiped his face and then reached out for Melanie, falling just short of her foot as she scooted into the corner. His shadow stretched almost to her ankle.

"All those years, your mother kept her secret from me." With a sudden lunge, he caught the hem of her jeans in his fist, pulling her out of the corner. "Then she died."

Melanie twisted away, but her father dragged her back into his embrace, hugging her so tightly it was far too difficult to even catch her breath as he sobbed against her shoulder. Great heaving sobs that threatened to crush her ribs. His arms wrapped tighter around her, clutching her as he cried.

"We celebrated your birthday last year, same as always, your mom and I," he said. "Within a week, she was dead and I was alone. I was lost again." He watched her, not releasing his hold. "And now you're here." He smiled and then squeezed still tighter. "Right where you always belonged."

Melanie tried to catch her breath, tried to push him far enough away to move freely, but there was no gentleness in his hold on her. She tried to speak as he wiped his tears on her shoulder, but all that came out was a whisper. "I can't breathe."

He looked up then, the smile gone and replaced by something far less comforting. "Sorry," he said as he released his hold. She took deep gasping breaths until the room stopped spinning. "I'm sorry for everything."

But even as he apologized, the shadow he cast seemed to reach out for her, drowning her with his presence.

"Chocolate, with buttercream icing," he said, taking her hand between his two large calloused palms. "She'd bake it and then we'd sing 'Happy Birthday.' Chocolate was always your favorite, right?"

Melanie nodded, but he wasn't paying attention. He let go of her only long enough to brush the hair out of her face. "Just like her, you know? Always so beautiful."

Then he smiled a great big smile, ear to ear, exposing his

teeth and gums as he stared at her with bloodshot eyes. A cloud of alcohol-tainted breath washed her skin as he spoke.

"This year was different," he said. "On your birthday, I had to bake the cake myself. It didn't taste very good. Not like hers. Then I went through all the old pictures of you. It wasn't enough. I wanted more of you. Needed it. So I pulled out everything of your mother's. All of the stuff I'd packed up after she died."

His voice rambled on, slurring every once in a while as it grew in intensity. "She'd put all of the pictures on the computer, so I turned on a slide show and got drunk and ate all of that crappy chocolate cake, but it didn't matter. Nothing mattered at all. She was dead and you were gone and all the beer in the world wasn't going to change that."

He leaned closer, his shadow covering her, and pulled her into his embrace again, barely leaving her room to breathe as he rested his head on her shoulder and kept talking.

"The slide show ended as the last picture, you playing some game on Mom's computer, faded away—and I remembered how you used to send me silly emails from her account. Nothing more than a word or two I'm sure Mommy helped you with. So I signed in. Her account was still active and filled with crap. In one of the folders, I found all the emails you'd sent me. I must have cried for hours, reading those."

He wiped his nose with his sleeve. "It was like I was talking to you, waiting for your reply. Then I started deleting all the random emails. That's when I found it." His eyes turned brittle and he tightened his grip. "One email, all it said was 'MOK.' Like the word 'mock' without a *C*."

The shadows spun around her, dancing with the wisps of her hair, and Melanie closed her eyes to block out the sight of their dance. Her father's voice scratched against her ears, the drunken slur darker and heavier now as he sniffled and continued on.

"I stared at it, thinking it had to be spam, right? It made no sense, so I figured I'd just delete it and keep going." He laughed, a hard, terrifying sound that caused her to flinch as he squeezed just a little harder. "Then I said it out loud. Go on, Melanie. Say it out loud."

She opened her eyes, jerking back when she realized he was staring at her, his face mere inches away, close enough for her to count the individual gray hairs on his chin. His too-warm breath crashed over her, and for a moment she worried whether second-hand alcoholism worked the same way as second-hand smoke.

"Say it," he said, the words clipped and short.

She took a deep breath. Her mouth was so dry, no matter how much she licked her lips it didn't help. After another deep breath, she swallowed and then tried to speak. "Mok."

"No, spell it."

"*M*," she said, then, "*O, K.*"

He smiled and placed a hard kiss on her cheek. "That's when it hit me," he said. "*M, O, K. M* stands for 'Melanie,' see? 'Melanie's okay.' It made perfect sense in my drunken state. So I searched through her email. Guess what I found?"

Melanie shook her head, simply trying to breathe.

"On your birthday the year before, the same email. 'MOK.' That's when I stopped drinking. Cold turkey." He pushed her away and stood up, pacing in her little room as Melanie crawled into the corner of her bed. "The next day, I hired a PI to trace the email. I bet you can figure out what I found. An anonymous email from an IP address at a library in Dothan, Alabama. I quit my job and sat in that damn library for almost a month, waiting every day until you and that family entered."

Her father walked to the side of the bed, towering above her, and when he reached for her she flinched. "I wanted to go up to you. I knew it was you; you look so much like her." He rested his weight on the edge of the mattress again as he stroked her hair, stray strands flying every which way and sending shadows dancing against the sheets. His fingers lingered on her cheeks. "Such pale skin. I never wanted to stop touching her and those shiny lips that never smiled often enough. She was so beautiful."

He closed his eyes, lost in his memories, and then wrapped Melanie in his embrace, holding her so tightly it was almost impossible to breathe. The shadows reached out to her, but when she reached back they turned out to be just ordinary shadows, nothing more than a trick of the light.

TWENTY-THREE

I finished eating as Max sat down with his lunch. On the other side of the room, Melanie turned around, and I stared down at the table to block out the sight.

Caitlin hid behind her hair as Max leaned against her shoulder. "All your hair's blocking my view," he said.

"You're not supposed to be reading this," she said, covering her page with her arms.

"Wasn't looking at the poetry." His bright smile faded as he cast his chin toward the table where Melanie was eating. "Any news?"

I glanced away before she caught me looking and turned to the corners of the cafeteria, where the shadows melted around the numerous students wandering through them.

"No," I said, and nothing more. What else was there to say?

"Do anything over the weekend?" he asked.

I shook my head, but he wasn't speaking to me.

"It's like talking to a wall," he said, reaching out to tap Caitlin on the shoulder.

She brushed her long hair off her face. "What?"

"I said, 'do anything over the weekend?'" He smiled, leaning forward to try to sneak a peek at the paper in front of her.

Caitlin covered it up once more before answering. "Hilton Head with my parents and Sidney."

"Sidney?" Max scooted just a little closer to her.

"My sister," Caitlin said, holding her hand in the air four feet up or so. "About this tall, brunette. Looks nothing like me. Looks a little like you, though."

"You do anything?" I asked Max when he stopped laughing.

"Just another fun time on the Georgia coast," he said. "Spent most of yesterday on my front lawn, watching cop cars driving around."

"I heard about that," I said.

Caitlin flicked her pencil against her teeth. "They were saying a girl went missing in Bluffton last week, too. Pretty much ruined the weekend, since my mom never let us out of her sight." She shivered once, then scribbled something in her notebook

"That's three," Max said, counting on his fingers. "Sue Chapman here in Savannah. Ellen Marie whatever her name is, near where I live." He glanced at Caitlin for a name.

"Not sure," she said. "It was a vacation. I wasn't paying much attention to the news."

"Seems like a lot," he said.

For a moment, the shadows shifted around me, fluorescent lights flickering above the room. "Four," I said. "Heard someone talking earlier about an Amber Alert issued in Waycross. Not sure who it's for, but that would make four."

"Might not all be related," Max said. "My dad was talking to one of the cops, who told him they were searching for a 'suspicious male.'" He made air quotes around the words with a shake of his head.

"I think they're looking for an older woman in Waycross," I said.

Logan passed by on his way toward Melanie, dragging his lunch bag across the table so it bumped into my tray. "Casper is a suspicious male," he said before turning to Caitlin. "And with all that hair, I guess that would make Max a suspicious female."

"Takes one to know one," Caitlin said, but Logan had already left, still laughing.

"Don't let him get to you," Max said to me as Logan sat next to Melanie.

"He's an ass," Caitlin added, before turning to her notebook and letting her hair fall around her face.

I wanted to stop watching them as Logan reached over the table, fingers playing an imaginary piano on Melanie's arm. I wanted to block out the sight of her laughing at something he said, brushing her hair back to smile at him. I stood, pushing the table hard enough to make the legs squeak on the linoleum.

I was almost out of the cafeteria when Melanie grabbed my shoulder. "Did you go?" she asked, the words hissed out.

I shook my head and her fingers gripped tighter.

"You promised," she said.

Logan walked between us, breaking her grip. "Sorry, Casper, didn't see you there." He smiled at me with those blank eyes. Then he looked at Melanie. "I'm heading to practice. Feel like working?"

She turned to him, flashing a brief smile. "I'll be right there."

Logan winked at me before heading toward the music wing.

"It's not what you think," she said.

"You have no idea what I think," I said, struggling to keep the hurt out of my voice and failing miserably. The shadow trailed out of the cafeteria behind me like a lost cat, weaving in and out of my legs, screaming her sad, sad song.

"You need to tell the police," Melanie said.

"Tell them what?" I asked. "Tell them how?"

She shrugged and walked away, the harsh institutional lighting creating shadows that followed her down the hall. Too large a part of me wanted to follow, wanted to stop her and bring her back to my side, wanted to keep her from singing with Logan, from being alone with him.

From kissing him.

TWENTY-FOUR

At work, they stopped the trolley in front of the Marshall House and the guide invited me to talk to the tourists again. Some even took my picture or asked me to pose with them. No one was talking about missing girls or police blockades and it made for a relatively relaxing tour, just searching Haunted Savannah for ghosts and spirits. I kept pointing out the window as I spoke, sending my own shadow dancing across the tourists, but if anyone felt anything, they didn't mention it.

When the tour was done, I took off in the Neon and drove south, back to Fort McAllister, to Savage Island, to the bones. The sun was setting, causing shadows to flicker around me as the chilly breeze blew off the ocean. The smell of the marshes was strong with salt and a subtle undercurrent of stagnant water. Once more, I took out my sketchbook, inviting the shadow to draw with me, but even though every inch of my exposed skin burned and the screaming drove me to my knees, the paper remained blank.

Without the shadow as a guide, I drew anyway. A rough outline of a tomb, a skull that lacked passion and seemed disconnected from the clichéd scene around it. A little girl knelt in prayer at the side of an empty hole. I waited for her to turn around, to see me, to acknowledge my presence somehow.

But there was no special smile meant for me alone, no acknowledgement at all. I was merely an observer and she was just a drawing, blank and boring.

I listened to the wailing, trying to understand, to pick out individual words or even just syllables, but it was as pointless as it had always been. The screams were only screams, no rhyme or reason; anguish and agony without end, without meaning. I searched the flames, struggling to find something in the fire clamoring within, some semblance of communication as embers floated away. But I was damned. I had always been damned. And I had long since given up on any hope of heaven.

I reached into my backpack, past the schoolbooks and the pencils, to pull out the bunched-up T-shirt at the bottom. Carefully unwrapping the fabric, I held the tiny skull in my palms, staring deeply into those empty eye sockets.

I wiped my eyes and then washed the bone with my tears. A rough breeze whistled through, creating a hissing from the skull, and I brought it to my face, close enough to smell the dirt clinging to it. And then closer still, so my lips rested on her forehead for an instant, nothing more, tasting the soil of Savannah.

For a moment I believed I heard the laughter of a little

girl, but it was just the wind ripping at the leaves. I stared at the skull, so small and delicate, and spoke as quietly as possible; not even a whisper, nothing more than a half-formed prayer.

"Melanie," I said, placing one more kiss on her forehead, imagining the soft hair and the soft skin and the soft eyes I'd drawn so many times. Wondering, once more, who had buried this innocent child here. "It's time to go home."

The sound echoed to silence, fading as though it had never existed.

"To your mother."

The fire dissipated, the heat leaching away and leaving me to shiver in the chilly autumn night.

"To your father."

The moon sent pale shadows of bare branches around the clearing. So many shadows, dancing in the breeze. A dozen of them or more twirling around me, silent and cold and achingly beautiful.

"It's time to find out who killed you," I said, once again picking up the pencil and turning to a blank page in my sketchbook.

A cloud passed by in front of the moon, dropping the clearing into darkness before it continued on its way, and the shadows reappeared, dancing and spinning. They surrounded me, embraced me, but remained quiet and cool as my hand flew across the paper. One enormous tree covered almost the entire page, broken and dying and sad, barely strong enough to stand upright. Branches hung to the ground, waiting to fall off and disappear.

And in front of that glorious, fading tree, a circle of tombstones pushed out of the ground, each with a tiny angel carved on the top of it. And each angel was as damaged and dying as the tree. A missing wing here, a cracked halo there. So small, the angels staring out at me, waiting for me as though I was the one who might fix them, might save them somehow.

But I was helpless and fragile and lost as I drew each one, each melancholy face on each precious angel on each ruined tombstone. My tears fell onto my sketchbook, wetting the paper, creating small puddles of distortion on the picture. I kept drawing through the futility and despair, shading those angels so they almost lived and breathed despite their injuries.

In front of each tombstone, a small hand, the bones so very delicate, reached up, reached out, reached for me, casting vibrant, vicious, feminine shadows across the ground.

For one brief moment, my eyes closed, blocking out the vision of what I'd drawn, denying the existence of all those broken angels, and the clearing was still and silent. The shadow was calm, wrapping herself around me in the moonlight, trailing tendrils of darkness over my skin to wrap me in her warm embrace.

Instead of howling, there was laughter and joy and the promise and hope of heaven in her eternal touch. She kissed me, then, my lips on fire as the moon shone on us, dancing and twirling on her grave.

TWENTY-FIVE

After school the next day, the Neon started on the second try and I drove down Bull Street to Precinct Three of the Savannah-Chatham Metropolitan Police. The small brick-and-glass building looked as though it had once been a dry cleaner's, maybe in the early 1970s or so. Perhaps a brief stint as a Chinese take-out restaurant. The building was dwarfed by a large oak tree trailing Spanish moss, its shadows floating on the breeze.

I parked across the street and sat there, watching the cars drive by and holding my backpack on my lap. Despite the late autumn chill I felt too hot, sweating while just looking at the police station. The shadow had been quiet and distant ever since we'd left the clearing, no longer fighting my need to tell someone about the bones. And that's what it was—a need kindled, a need to find justice for Melanie

Elizabeth Bellemeade. To find her killer, to avenge the death of my best friend.

To do something, anything. For so long I'd been power-less. I'd been six years old. What could I have done? I'd turned around. I'd counted to one hundred. But other than that, I'd done nothing. For years, I did nothing. Even when I told people, begging them to believe Melanie was there, with me, no one ever listened. Not my parents, not my classmates, no one.

Worst of all, they were right. The shadow wasn't Mela-nie. But it didn't matter. The shadow was my best friend. I'd spent every day of the past ten years with her. This was my chance to save Melanie the way she'd always saved me.

The day I turned thirteen, my mother made me invite my entire class to a party at my house. She bought childish invitations and forced me to give them out, covered in color-ful balloons.

The day after I handed them out, I found a stack in the garbage can in the library at school. They had drawn faces on all of the balloons, turning them into cartoon characters, mocking me. They'd turned them into ghosts.

No one came to the party.

That night, hours after my parents had put me to bed, I listened to the shadow scream until I couldn't take it any lon-ger. I tiptoed down the stairs, into the kitchen, and picked up the phone. The night I turned thirteen, I called 911 to tell the police the truth.

They sent a bored detective and then, after waking my parents and humoring me by listening to my tale of ghosts and shadows, they sent child protective services the next day.

Just to check in. To make sure I'd been taking my medicine, to see if I needed more.

"A terrible tragedy," they said. "Life gets better" and "We're here for you."

But it was more than a tragedy, and sometimes life has funny ways of getting better and only the shadow was ever there for me. Not Melanie, not my parents; no one but the shadow.

I crossed the street, watching the Spanish moss tangle in the branches. Despite the shadows flowing along the pavement, I wasn't all that surprised to see that once again, I cast no shadow. For this, for now, I was alone.

Inside the police station I hesitated long enough to be noticed.

"May I help you?" a woman officer asked as I stood there.

I swallowed, the words floating free and fading away. Then I closed my eyes and nodded. Opened them and looked her square in the face: kind brown eyes beneath a short shock of blonde hair. She wore an equally kind smile, infinitely patient, as though dealing with hesitant kids were just another part of the job. Which, come to think of it, probably was.

"I wanted to talk to someone about some bones," I said, the words tripping over themselves in their rush to get out. "I found them out near Fort McAllister."

She smiled just a little wider and gave me one of those "just a minute" gestures while she picked up the phone on her desk. "Detective," she said, "there's a young man here for you."

She turned to me and pointed to a row of hard plastic seats. "Someone will be right with you, okay?" she said.

I took a seat, clutching my backpack in front of me.

Too many minutes passed, as I squirmed on the uncomfortable chair, before a middle-aged man, grey hair peppering the black, appeared. His tie was loosely knotted, as though he'd been pulling at it to keep it from his neck. I knew the feeling—the same feeling I had whenever I had to get dressed for some family affair and my throat felt too constricted. The shadow hated it, ripping at the fabric until we were able to breathe again.

"Detective McGuire," he said, holding out a hand, his grip firm and quick. "And you are?"

"Richard Harrison."

"This way, Richard." He spun around, his shoes squeaking on the tiles as he lead me through a maze of old metal desks. A couple of officers glanced up as we walked by, but other than that, no one paid us much attention. When we reached a desk that was only one spot removed from having part of a window view, the detective pulled out a chair and dragged it over, motioning me to sit.

He sat next to me, flipped an already-open notebook to an empty page, and wrote my name at the top. Then he studied me with the same bored eyes as the officer who'd come to my house on my thirteenth birthday. "Address?" he asked, writing my answer beneath my name. "Phone?"

When all the preliminaries were done, he let out a

deep sigh, rolling his shoulders and reading what little he'd already written.

"What can I help you with, Richard?" he asked.

I took a deep breath, missing the kind face of the woman who'd first helped me. "I found some bones," I said, the words hurried out of me, eager to be spoken. "Buried near Fort McAllister."

On his notebook, Detective McGuire wrote "bones" and the name of the Fort and nothing else. When he finished writing, the bored look had grown. "Lots of bones found around here lately," he said. "Mostly animal. Especially out on the islands. Best thing you can do is call it in and we'll get them checked out, make sure everything's okay, okay?"

The entire time his head was nodding, as though this was the eighth time today he'd given this speech. Judging by the blockade on Broughton Street the other night during the ghost tour, it just might have been.

He leaned forward, his hand outstretched to shake good-bye. The motion caught the fluorescent lights and sent a shadow across the floor. The shadows around the room came to life, spinning toward me and I was thirteen again, helpless, powerless.

I took a deep breath and reached for my backpack, pulling it into my lap. I ignored his outstretched hand and put my sketchbook on the edge of his desk. I took out the small T-shirt-wrapped bundle and placed it into the detective's palm.

"Well, that'll save some time, I guess," he said, gently unwrapping it.

As the last folds of fabric fell away and the harsh fluorescent lighting shone on the tiny human skull, the look of boredom disappeared from his face as though I'd pulled a gun on him.

He stared at the skull and then slowly, oh so slowly, raised bright, intense eyes, drilling into me for a very long moment. Then he turned to the skull again, reaching to the phone without looking at it. The background noises around us faded as one after another people noticed the skull he was holding.

"Captain," he said into the phone, "you're going to want to see this."

A number of other officers walked over as Detective McGuire gently placed the skull on his desk, handling it only with the T-shirt it had been wrapped in. He removed purple latex gloves from a desk drawer and pulled them on, only then touching the jawline of the skull.

From the corner office, an older man came out, his tie perfectly knotted. The sea of officers surrounding McGuire's desk parted until his shadow fell on the skull.

"It looks old," McGuire said without glancing at the captain.

"Where was it found?" he asked, turning from the detective to me and back again.

"Richard Harrison," McGuire said, introducing me. "Says he found it buried by Fort McAllister."

"Go there often?" the captain asked.

I shrugged, thinking of how I'd planned to answer all the questions I figured I'd be asked. "Just hiking, looking for things to draw. Went there for a field trip once. Found a clearing the other day."

"Do you make a habit of digging holes in state parks?"

"No." I shook my head, the shadow within uneasy and jittery. "Just at the base of this tree, the ground was all torn up, like an animal had been scavenging. I was going to sit down, take a break, when I saw that." I pointed at the skull, the empty eye sockets staring straight at me.

While I was talking, another pair of officers came in. The captain pointed at the skull. "Document that, then take it downtown. I'll contact them before you get there." Then he turned to Detective McGuire. "Why are you two still here?" he asked.

"Do you have a car here?" the detective asked.

"Across the street."

"I'll follow you, okay?"

"Where are we going?" I asked, but even as the words were on their way out of my mouth, I knew it was one of the single stupidest questions I'd ever given voice to. Detective McGuire knew it, too, and didn't answer as we walked out the door.

"Don't speed," he said, leaving me at my Neon and heading to his own unmarked police car.

———

By the time we reached the island, dusk had settled over the ocean, spreading a sea of shadows around us. The night sounds of the marshes were far too loud, angry at being disturbed and interrupted. The bright flashlight of Detective McGuire far outshone the flash app on my phone, sending dizzying shadows in circles as we hiked the fading deer track. In the clearing, the giant oak tree dwarfed the two of us as I shone my light at the base.

The detective walked around, shining his flashlight on the ground where leaves had covered the digging I'd done. "You filled the hole back in?" he asked, turning to shine his light directly at me.

I raised my hands, covering my eyes and casting a shadow on my own face. The heat lingered on my skin, running across my lips.

"I thought I should," I said. "In case any more animals were around."

"Anything else?" he asked as he knelt in the mulch.

I shook my head but he wasn't looking. "No," I said. "I just wanted to do the right thing."

"You did," he said, and then leaned forward, shining the flashlight at the ground again. "Here?"

Again, he couldn't see my nod. "Yes, there."

Detective McGuire pulled out a small camera and took a couple of pictures before turning around to me. "Thanks, Richard," he said, brushing the loose dirt off his knees. "I'm going to call this in and get a team out here. Expect me to stop by your house in the next day or two." He gave me an odd sort of smile, almost apologetic. "I'm going to have more questions. For now, your picturesque little clearing is a crime scene, so I'm going to suggest you head home, okay?"

I took one last glance at the shadows dancing around us, flowing with the cool ocean breeze.

"You did good, Richard," he said, stretching his hand out once more.

His grip was just as firm as the first time, though not as abrupt.

"Thanks," I said.

"Thank you," he said as he stared into the branches of the tree, shining his flashlight on the broken and cracked bark.

I walked halfway down the deer track before turning around. The detective was still shining his flashlight at the branches, sending shadows into the sky.

TWENTY-SIX

"There's another one," Max said, sliding his tray along the table. It came to a stop in front of his seat.

I looked up as he arrived. Caitlin sat across from us.

"Another what?" I asked.

"Missing girl," Caitlin said from behind her hair. She pushed it aside long enough to take a bite of her sandwich, and then let it fall down.

"From Richmond Hill," Max said. "Second grader."

"That's, what?" Caitlin asked. "Five?"

Both Max and I nodded. "In a month," he said. "Might be a copycat."

"Doesn't matter. I still have to pick Sidney up after school every day now," Caitlin said. "My mom's a little freaked."

"I think everyone's a little freaked," Max said. "If you want, I'll go with you."

She cocked her head to the side, far enough for the hair to

fall away from her face, exposing a bright smile. "I'd like that," she said. "Thanks."

When Caitlin turned to her lunch, Max caught my eye and winked before pointing to Melanie, who was walking toward us. Melanie's hair had been left free, twisting and curling around her neck, bouncing with a life of its own with each breath she took. Her eyes retained a hint of fear as she spoke with me, but it was far less than it had been.

"Well?" she asked, the word almost lost in the chaos of the cafeteria.

A couple of tables away, Logan looked over, his blank stare never leaving us. I turned from him, from her, and got up, threading my way through the crowded lunchroom, knowing she was following behind. The hallways were deserted but promised little privacy, so I led us to a stairwell and sat in the corner, waiting for her to join me.

She stood across from me, not taking a seat. "Well?" she asked again.

"I went," I said. "I even led them to the clearing."

I heard the breath leave her as she slid down the wall to sit on the edge of the step. "Are you okay?" she asked.

With a shrug, I shook my head. "It's out of my hands now. They said it seemed 'old,' so I guess that's good."

"Did you tell them about ... " Her words trailed to silence before she quietly finished. "Me?"

"No," I said. "Just told them I'd been hiking."

"Thanks," she said. "I guess."

"You're welcome, I guess."

"They still want to talk to me," she said. "About the whole

'coming back from the dead' thing." Her laugh was weak and short-lived, but it was something at least. "I don't even know what to tell them. The truth? That my father locked me in a box? That my mom was so afraid he'd hurt me she hid me in Alabama?" She ran her fingers through her hair, tugging them free with a sigh. "Maybe they'll just forget about me."

"Maybe," I said. "Even the news people seem to have moved on. That's a good thing, right?"

She attempted to smile, succeeding only halfway if that. "I don't think I believe in 'good things' any longer. I think I stopped believing a very long time ago."

"Melanie," I said, but after her name I ran out of things to say.

"No," she said. "Just let it go."

I tried to think of a reply to that, but there was nothing but a vast emptiness swallowing me, hollow and lonely.

"About Logan—" she said after a long silence.

"I don't want to know," I said, cutting her off before she said anything else. I stared at the floor, counting the tiles.

"There's nothing to tell."

Along the edges of the linoleum, the shadows flowed out of the corners, stretching a welcoming embrace around me. I sighed with the contact, with the first touch of a comforting presence filling the desolation within.

"She's here," Melanie said, quiet and so far away. "You change when she's with you."

"I'm sorry," I said.

"Me too."

And then she was gone, walking out of the stairwell and

leaving me alone with the shadow, scorching my lips with a lingering kiss.

———————

"Again?" Logan asked, picking out a simple tune on the keys.

Melanie sighed, leaning against the wavy foam wall. The door was closed, but some faint sounds of the school managed to seep through the glass window. She took a deep breath, then another, before Logan began to play.

The notes came so easily, floating on the air, but there was something mechanical about it all. No matter how much she related to the song, loving the lyrics and feeling each and every piece of the music, there was always something missing. Something she didn't know how to define.

At the piano, Logan kept shaking his head, saying "No" under his breath as he played. "You'll never leave the chorus like this," he said. "Maybe second from the left in the ensemble, if you go the theatrical route."

Melanie let the music fade, let the song die, and slid down the wavy wall to rest on the floor. "You think I'd even try to do this for a living?" she asked with a quick, sharp laugh.

"You're here, aren't you?" he answered. "Savannah Arts to Oberlin or Julliard or something. If you didn't want to sing, you could be at some other crappy high school around here taking Latin right now."

He walked over and sat next to her. Melanie scooted away, and he smiled at the movement.

"Afraid of me?" he asked.

"No," she said, but didn't move closer. "I meant to tell you my dad said no to going on a date, though."

"He does realize we're more alone here than we'd be at a movie, right?" Logan said, leaning over to bump her shoulder with his. "Want to try again?"

Melanie shook her head. "There's no point," she said. "There's never a point to it."

"Do you play?" he asked, gesturing toward the piano.

"No," she said. "A little guitar, but that's about it. I started singing when I was seven or so. Just never felt right playing an instrument."

"I started when I was born, I think. After my dad left, I was pretty much on my own, so it was just me and our broken piano."

"Where was your mom?"

"She was never all there," he said. "Then it got worse when he left. I'd hide in my room, practicing on a battery-powered keyboard for hours. Still do, actually. Just one more reason I drive so far to come here. Well, that and the company." He brought one hand to her chin, turning her to him. "They're fading," he said, tilting her head to expose her neck.

She tried to push him away, but he kept his fingers on her long enough to place a kiss at the base of her throat, where the bruises had been.

"What's the deal with Casper?" he asked, his breath warm on her skin.

Melanie backed up, wrapping her arms around herself. "Nothing," she said. "And even if there was something, my father would still say no. It isn't just you I can't date."

"I think there's something." Logan stood and went to the piano bench to pound out a harsh rhythm that dominated the small practice room. "Now, sing."

And she sang. And he shook his head until she couldn't take it anymore and ran from the room. He continued playing, his glorious music following her down the hall, mocking her.

TWENTY-SEVEN

Somewhere, music played. A lullaby repeating over and over, so far away it echoed in the darkness.

"It's time for tea," a voice said, briefly interrupting the music.

She struggled to open her eyes as the heavy, damp fabric was lifted, blinking against the bright light of candles surrounding her. Nothing was in focus, little made sense; merely shadows flickering in and out of sight with each blink. She strained to wipe her eyes, but her hands didn't move, and when she wriggled her fingers, they didn't budge. Her head flopped to the side and she tried to see her arms. They were nothing but thin, pale shapes in the distance. She blinked and her hands came into focus.

Rope was wrapped around her wrists, trailing to the ceiling, far beyond the reach of the candlelight. She blinked again, until the table in front of her came into focus as well. A single china cup on a small saucer sat in front of her. Something that might have been a sigh echoed, and she fought to turn her head far enough to the side to see more of the table.

Four more cups, on four more saucers, circled the candles in the middle, and, as she blinked, she saw the other girls from the cages. Four more girls, all with long brown hair, so alike they could have been sisters. Four more pairs of brown eyes blinked at her from gaunt, haunted faces. Four more pairs of hands tied to four more pairs of ropes trailing to the ceiling. Four more girls costumed in pretty dresses covering dirty clothes. Four more heads flopping back and forth, fighting to escape and failing.

"Time for tea." The voice came again, but try as she might to pierce the flickering darkness surrounding them, there was nothing to see in the shadows.

As the ropes tightened, her right hand rose in front of her, the fingers drooping like dead weight. The squeals and squeaks of a metal pulley above her thundered through the room as the ropes lifted her arm, slowly moving it until her fingers bumped against the cup. Liquid spilled over the rim but she couldn't feel the burn. Couldn't feel anything.

She could only watch the wisps of steam floating from the cup to the ceiling, where the ropes disappeared in shadows and rusty pulleys squealed in agony as the same lullaby played one more time. Could only watch as all of their hands bounced repeatedly off their cups, spilling tea and sending flickering shadows dancing around the room.

TWENTY-EIGHT

No matter how long I stared at it, the canvas remained disturbingly blank. The shadows were quiet and calm even though I was raging inside, gripping the paintbrush with such force I feared it would break. For a moment I anticipated the solid crack of the wooden brush, sought the ache it would cause as it stabbed through my skin and sent splinters into my palm. But the brush refused to cooperate and remained whole. Mocking me, taunting my inability to create as those words repeated in my memory:

When he kissed me.

It was impossible to escape the image of Logan kissing Melanie. It squeezed out every other emotion, every other thought until all that remained was a blank canvas.

I remained there, staring, hours later, after my mom got home from work. When the doorbell rang and she called my name, I knew, without a doubt, Melanie was there.

I was wrong.

Detective McGuire stood in the living room, towering over my mom, who watched me with a strange, foreign look in her eyes.

"Sorry to bother you, ma'am," he said, tilting his head to her before turning to me. "I hope I'm not here at a bad time?"

She glared at me and the shadow circled the room, uneasy and restless. "There's a good time?" my mother asked, taking a seat on the edge of the couch where Melanie had sat that first night. "Am I supposed to know why you're here?"

"I was going to tell you," I said, sitting as far from her as possible while still remaining in the same room.

"Tell me what?" she asked. And then, "I'm sorry, Detective, I'm not sure what's going on here."

"Richard," McGuire said, once more taking out his notebook as he sat. "Perhaps it might be best if you started at the very beginning."

The shadow burrowed into me, hiding from the world without a sound. "I go to Savannah Arts Academy," I said, looking at the detective so I wouldn't have to face my mother. "I like to go hiking with my sketchbook. Just anywhere. Tybee, River Street. Wherever. Lately I've been going to the fort, wandering around. Searching for things to draw. The other night I went kind of late. It was dark, a lot more animals were around. That's when I found the clearing."

Detective McGuire leaned back and looked at my mom for a long moment. "And the bones?"

The question ripped a gasp from my mother, her harsh breath echoing in the small room. "Bones?" she asked.

"Just a skull," I said, as though that would make it all better. Which, of course, it didn't.

"Not just a skull," the detective said, his notebook ignored in his lap. "Fourteen skulls."

The shadow exploded, breaking apart into smaller and smaller pieces until more than a dozen voices echoed through me. They were shy and brave and hesitant and aggressive and screaming such a terrible, lonely scream it was almost impossible to breathe. As their cries overwhelmed me I cried out, screeching to wake the dead or damn the guilty or punish the innocent. I bellowed. I burned. And then, sweet blessed glorious heaven, there was absolute silence as I collapsed to the ground.

"Richard!" the detective yelled, from so far away he might just as well have stayed silent. Then he rested his fingers on my throat. I begged him silently to squeeze and squeeze until everything ceased, but just as quickly he let go.

"He's breathing," he said, and all I wanted was for him to be wrong. Surely I couldn't be alive. I so didn't want to be alive.

Gentle and tender, the shadows wrapped themselves around me with a quiet warmth. And then, with one final, blazing kiss, they let me go.

My eyes blinked open, struggling to focus. Detective McGuire was sitting on the floor next to me, my mom on the phone with my father, telling him to come home from work as soon as possible.

"Are you okay?" McGuire asked as he handed me a glass of water.

I nodded, rising far enough to take a sip.

"Richard?" my mom asked in her maternal voice, holding her hand to my cheek and shaking her head.

"I'm fine," I said, then drank the rest of the water.

"I'm sorry," Detective McGuire said. "I wasn't thinking."

"No kidding—" my mom said, but I cut her off.

"It's okay, just a little overwhelming," I said. "I wanted to know. I still want to know."

"That's pretty much all we know so far," McGuire said. "DNA testing will take time. I just wanted to thank you again for helping out. And I wanted you to hear it from me before you saw it on the news."

"Thanks," I said as the detective stood to leave. He was halfway to the door before I was able to find the strength to stand and follow him. "Detective McGuire." I reached out to stop him from leaving.

He turned to me, staring at my fingers where they rested on his arm. He looked at my mother, and then he rested his hand on my forehead. "You're burning up," he said. "Are you sure you're okay? I can call an ambulance."

"I'm fine."

"His temperature is normally high," my mother said. "We've gotten used to it."

"Was there something else, Richard?"

"The other skulls," I said, rushing the words out. "Are they new?"

"No. Least as far as I can tell, they all appear to be old, but, as I said, it'll take some time to figure everything out. Thank you for everything. If you have any more questions..." He gave my mom his business card, shook my hand, and left.

I closed my eyes as we stood in the living room, and for a long while my mom just let me stand there. The shadows were quiet, waiting for something, but I had no idea what they might be waiting for.

"Richard," my mother said after the silence stretched out too long. "You should have told us."

"I'm sorry," I said, because those were the words she wanted to hear. "I will, the next time I discover a mass grave, okay?" I even laughed, but it was a pitiful attempt, dying out moments after it started.

Before my mother said anything else, I walked to my room, pulled out my phone, and called Melanie. The shadow caressed my arms and hands and every other inch of exposed skin, trailing haunted kisses even as I was speaking on the phone.

"Hi," I said.

"Hi."

"Are you busy?"

"Not really," she said. "Why?"

"The police just left."

"What happened?"

"Can you come over?"

For a long moment there was nothing but the quiet whisper of her breath on the phone. "Please?" I asked.

"Will she be there?"

"She won't hurt you," I said, my lips on fire from her kiss. "I promise."

"I'll be right there." And then she was gone, and the shadow and I were alone once more.

TWENTY-NINE

I turned on every light in my room, shining the brightness into every corner to drive out every shadow. Only then did I think Melanie would feel safe, or hope she'd feel safe, at least.

When the doorbell rang, I let her in and led her down the hall. Light poured out from beneath my door, almost blinding as we entered and I shut it behind us.

"Little bright," she said, "don't you think?"

I smiled but it didn't quite take. "I figured it might help."

"It does." She sat in the chair, leaning against my desk and staring at all the pictures lining the walls, vivid in the blaze of illumination. "But it's not necessary."

"Are you okay?" I asked.

"We're okay, if that's what you're asking," she said. "I guess."

I sat on the edge of the bed, facing her. Beneath the glow of all those lights, stray strands of her long hair fired sparks of copper as they curled around her shoulders, and it was difficult to tear my eyes from the curves of her neck and the memories of bruises.

"The police?" she asked, turning from me to study the closest painting.

"They found more skulls in the clearing," I said.

She spun to me, the chair squeaking with the motion. "How much is 'more'?"

"Fourteen."

She gasped, and the word hung in the air like a curse. "Fourteen?"

I leaned forward to reach out to her, but the shadow flared, locking my arms at my side.

"The missing girls?" she asked.

"No. They think they've all been there awhile."

"And Melanie?"

"They're running DNA tests," I said. "No names so far."

"Thanks," she said after a long silence.

"For what?"

"For going to the police." She wiped her tears away with a sniffle. "For everything."

"Thank you," I said. "For making me go."

Her laugh was little more than a sigh, but when she looked at me, there was at least the barest hint of a smile. "This wasn't how I pictured our reunion, you know?"

"What?" I said, hoping vainly for levity and obviously failing. "You weren't expecting ghosts?"

"No. I don't know what I was expecting, but it wasn't this."

"I know."

She scooted the chair a little closer to the bed, close enough to touch. "I'm not sure I'll ever get used to how warm you are," she said, trailing her fingers on my arm. "She's here, isn't she?"

I nodded, silent.

"I always thought it would be just you and me, together," she said, "the way it was before I left." Her shoulders drooped and her hand slid to rest against the mattress. "I dreamed we'd pick up just where we left off, playing hide-and-seek, but this time I'd let you find me. I always wanted you to find me."

"Did you think I would still be six years old?" I asked, fighting to keep the heat of the shadow out of my voice. "That I'd still be standing there with my eyes closed, counting to one hundred?"

Melanie closed her own eyes and turned from me. "No," she said, so quiet I barely heard the word. "I just wanted us to still be six. To still be playing hide-and-seek in my backyard. To still be best friends."

"We're not six anymore."

"I know." Tears drew pale tracks along her cheeks. "But I can wish, can't I?"

"I've been wishing for a decade now," I said.

"For what?"

I slid off the edge of the mattress, landing on my knees in front of her. Her fingers were shaking as I ran my thumb across her palm. "I wished for you, Melanie. I never stopped wishing for you."

I closed the distance between us until she was so close I felt her cool breath against my too-warm skin. The beating, living pulse of her where my thumbs rested on her wrists. Smelled the vanilla cream freshness of her shampoo, the cinnamon mint crispness of her toothpaste. The strawberry softness of her lips.

And then, the shadows were gone. The heat I'd always known melted away and I shivered in the sudden chill, trembling in the overwhelming loneliness of me.

Beneath my hands, however, Melanie's skin turned to ice—colder than that, colder than anything I'd ever imagined. Her eyes slammed open, wide with fear. She tried to speak—her whisper starting as a sigh, a moan, and then turning into something more, something sacred and profane, both a curse and a prayer. She screamed. She screamed and kept on screaming long after I took her freezing body into my arms and covered her mouth with my hands to lower the volume.

My parents rushed into my room while Melanie froze in my embrace, the shadows leaving me and disappearing inside of her.

THIRTY

"Call an ambulance!" My mother was yelling to make herself heard over the noise, but I reached out to my father to keep him from making the call.

"No," I said, shaking my head since there was no way for them to hear me. "Please, no."

"She's freezing," my mother said, resting a hand on Melanie's forehead.

"No," I said, again and again. Just a single word. "No."

My father shook me off and pulled his phone out of his pocket, but I swung my arm and knocked it to the ground.

"No," I said. "She'll be okay. Please, she'll be okay." I ran unsteady fingers through her hair, moving it out of her face and then brushing her tears away. "Shhh, Melanie," I whispered as she roared her wordless cry. I poured everything I had into her name, calling to her and to the shadows within.

"Trust me," I said. "She's going to be okay. It'll just take time."

"She needs a hospital," my mother said, bending to pick up my dad's phone before handing it to him.

"She needs me," I said. "Please, just go. She'll be okay, I promise."

They stared at me for a long time, but it didn't matter. I turned from my parents, turned to Melanie, crooning nonsense words to her in the hope that maybe, somehow, she heard my voice. When I looked, they were gone and the door was closed. We were alone—Melanie, the shadows, and I.

And then, as Melanie collapsed in my arms in sudden silence, it was just me. Alone, listening to her harsh breathing. I whispered her name, calling to her, calling her back to me.

The blinding brightness of my room pounded against my eyes, so I stretched as far as I was able and flipped the switch to turn off the overhead light. Then I ripped the cord out of the wall to unplug my desk lamp and plunge the room into darkness.

Her skin was ice cold as I held her face in my hands. As gently as possible I laid her on the ground and covered her with the blanket from my bed. I sat there, holding her frozen fingers, trying to keep her warm, waiting for her to wake. I watched her sleep, watched every breath move her body, verifying she still lived.

It was so quiet, her deep, gasping breaths the only sound as I prayed a wordless prayer for her to return, for her to open her eyes and smile. Around the room, countless drawings and paintings surrounded us like an audience of angels, reaching out to embrace us with skeletal arms.

She took one long, shuddering breath, her entire body shaking, and then the world stopped. She lay perfectly motionless for too many seconds to count.

"Melanie," I whispered.

Finally her eyes opened, staring at the ceiling without seeming to see it. Her body arched off the ground, her mouth wide open to inhale all the oxygen in the room. And then she began to breathe.

"Richard?" Her voice was a chorus, a symphony, a choir. Layered and rich and echoing on itself. It was her voice, and it was something else—something more, something shadowy.

She curled up, her muscles tightening and releasing. And then she turned to me, her eyes so very dark, lost in the shadows of the darkened room, and when she smiled, it was the most beautiful thing I'd ever seen.

"Richard," she said again, running her hands over her face as though it was something she'd never done before. Her thumb rested on her bottom lip, and, when she released the contact, she bit gently on her finger with a smile that was even more beautiful than the first.

"Richard," she said. My name was a caress as the chorus of voices called to me.

She reached for me, clutching so tightly as she fit her body to mine where we knelt in the middle of my darkened room, guarded by skeletal angels hiding in the shadows.

Her lips were soft as snow beneath mine, her skin icy to the touch. The pure cold of her bit deeply as she clung to me, as though I was a lifeline saving her from drowning, and perhaps I was. Perhaps I was her salvation, or she was mine. Savior or saint or sinner, or maybe I was merely drowning with her, sinking under the waves and breathing her in.

Cold radiated in waves from her lips; ice spread from the touch of her hands on my neck. Steam rose from where we touched, billowing to the ceiling.

When I opened my eyes, she was staring at me, her dark, dark eyes so very different than the dark blue I'd always drowned in. I tried to let go but she refused to let me escape, her fingers tightening where she held on too tightly.

I couldn't breathe, couldn't blink.

"Who are you?" I asked, as she stared into and through me with those dark, dark eyes. She smiled, and when she kissed me once more, the sweet cold of her lips eclipsed the stars.

I caressed her freezing skin and, fighting against my own desire to never stop kissing her, pushed her away. She clung to me. Her fingers twisted through my hair, pulling my lips to hers.

"I am … " She shivered, her body shaking in my arms. "I am … yours," she said, kissing me again, sharing her hunger with me. "I have always been yours." Again, that sparkling kiss, the overwhelming cold. "I will always be yours."

She wrapped herself around me and I counted to one hundred. I counted to one hundred and I turned around.

I turned around and she was there.

She had always been there.

So help me God.

"I am Melanie," she said, so many voices contained within those words, spoken out loud at last.

And then those dark, dark eyes lightened, becoming familiar and warm again. She shuddered against me, deep, gasping breaths fighting for air as the smile faded, replaced by something closer to confusion than passion.

Her voice was changed as well, no longer a chorus; it was hesitant and shy now, a pale echo of the vast symphony the shadow had spoken through. "I remember this," she said. "This is why I ran."

She stared at me, tears trailing glistening tracks on her beautiful face. "I remember her," she said. "I remember the cold. I just kept running, trying to keep warm. The screaming, so loud I couldn't understand the words. She was there, Richard. She made me run. She took me from you."

THIRTY-ONE

There was a quiet knocking on my door, followed by my mother's voice. "Richard? Melanie?" The door opened and she poked her head in.

In the shadowed darkness of my room, Melanie leaned away from me, her hair disheveled. I raised my arm to dim the bright light from the hallway.

"Are you okay?" my mother asked, looking from me to Melanie. "We can still take you to the ER, or call your dad."

"I'm okay," Melanie said. Her voice once more echoing with the shadow, her dark, dark eyes smiling.

"Me too," I added.

"If you need anything…" my mother said as she left, leaving the door wide open.

"Well," I said, sticking out my foot to swing the door shut, "that was uncomfortable."

Melanie laughed a bright laugh, bringing more light to

the bedroom than all the lamps combined. "That was wonderful," she said as she crawled into my lap and wrapped me in her arctic embrace.

"Melanie," I whispered.

Then her eyes changed again, the cold melting away as the thin sliver of light from the hallway cast a vibrant, vicious, feminine shadow across me. There was nothing but a quiet whisper, almost a moan, as the shadow came home. Wisps of steam trailed off my skin as Melanie kissed me even while the shadow was leaving her.

The cold of her lips was gone, though I figured she felt my own lips on fire against hers. Her eyes slowly closed and, against my mouth, she smiled.

"I should go," she said, placing a long, lingering kiss on my throat, right where my pulse beat against the skin. Her fingers wrapped in my hair.

"I know," I said, running my hands over her back, feeling the curves of her shoulder blades where they dipped down, tracing the outline of her bra strap through her shirt.

The shadow purred within as Melanie purred against me, her lips trailing upward, until I found myself lost in her kiss. Somewhere deep inside, the shadow sighed, and then, in the space between heartbeats, it surged between us, filling the room with steam as we drowned in a single, shared, eternal scream.

"That was—" she whispered.

"Yes," I whispered as well. "It was."

"I don't know what happens next with us," she said with a small smile. "My dad already said no to me dating Logan."

"Good," I said, and once more her laugh lit the room.

"Please don't."

"Don't what?"

"Don't worry about Logan," she said. "Or anyone else." She kissed me, so very gently, and then said "Ever" before kissing me one more time.

"I doubt he'll let me date you either," she added. "Not yet, at least. I think he's better this time, really he is. Even if he's drinking again." She closed her eyes. "But he's better, okay?"

"Okay."

"I really should be getting home." She pushed herself up and we stood in the middle of my room, the shadows swirling around and inside us.

"Are you going to be okay?" I asked.

"This is going to take some getting used to," she said with a slight smile. We walked to her car, waving to my parents on the way out of my house. I held her door open for her and closed it after her. Then I stood in the street, the shadows and I, as she drove away.

———

There were no news vans on her street, hadn't been since Sue Chapman had gone missing. The police had left a couple of messages, but she had yet to return them. One persistent reporter from the *Savannah Morning News* had actually left a note in their mailbox to contact him for an interview. Still, Melanie checked all around the house before pulling to the curb. She was about to get out when she noticed the front door was open, spilling light into the moonlit night.

She looked in the rearview mirror, then up and down the street again, but didn't see anyone. She'd only taken a couple of steps out of the car when the front door slammed shut, the sudden thud echoing though the air like a gunshot.

"Where is she?" someone female yelled from inside the house.

Through the window, she caught just a glimpse of long hair, with her father right behind. Again, a woman's voice cried out. "Where is she?"

If he said anything in response, Melanie wasn't able to hear it, but she heard something break, like glass exploding, followed by a high-pitched shriek. Then there was silence.

She scrambled to the car, dumping her purse out on the front seat in her rush to find her keys. She floored the gas and rocketed up the street. In the rearview mirror she saw someone stumble out of the house, right before she turned the corner.

She kept going, blowing through stop signs and red lights until her heartbeat steadied. Tears played tricks with her vision, and she wiped her eyes in order to focus on the road. Finally she pulled to a stop in an empty corner of the Savannah Mall parking lot, her breathing far too loud in the car.

She double-checked the locks and then closed her eyes, trying to calm down. The smell and feel of Richard lingered on her skin, the taste of him on her lips. But the woman's frantic cry—*Where is she?*—kept intruding, echoing with each beat of her heart.

Curled in the front seat, she tried to forget everything that had ever happened in her life. Tried to forget the lonely nights she'd cried out for Mommy only to remember Mommy had sent her away. Or the nights she'd dreamed of playing hide-and-seek with her best friend only to wake, still hidden and unfound, as the memories of him faded. Tried to forget, most of all, those miserable nights alone in her box, when the loneliness and fear threatened to break her into tiny pieces no one would ever be able to puzzle back together.

Sleep was a long time coming, but finally she lost herself in the seductive dream of a single, eternal kiss. It was interrupted by a bony hand wrapping around her, pulling her into a deep dark grave. In the glacial embrace of the bones and the dirt, she was no longer alone; the whispers of shadows sang a half-remembered lullaby.

THIRTY-TWO

She blinked against the bright pinpoint of light slicing through the darkness, pressing her against the bars of her cage. Somewhere far away, someone moaned. It might have been her. Every breath brought new sources of pain. Her lungs seized in a fit of coughing, causing her head to slam against the bars. But at least she was moving, her eyes blinking, opening at her own command.

The voice was closer now, echoes and echoes of it, as light bobbed up and down, cutting through the darkness. Then, for a moment that lasted no longer than a blink, the flashlight shone on another cage, another girl, throwing a violent shadow across the room.

"Stop squirming," someone said as they reached inside.

She blinked, but everything was out of focus, her head flopping to the side with another cough, and the flashlight beam bounced and sparkled in her vision.

"Hold her still," someone else said, the new voice also floating

through the darkness, coming out of the shadows to reach for her. "Hush, little one, this won't hurt at all."

And then the voices were silent for a blink, before the girl in the other cage yelled once and fell silent.

She squeezed her eyes closed as the beam of the flashlight swept past, the footsteps coming closer, coming for her. The door opened with a harsh metallic shriek and too many hands reached in.

"Time for your medicine," the voices said.

She squirmed, kicking out, but the kick had little strength behind it. She was too weak, too sick, too small compared to those giant hands grabbing her ankles, pulling her out of the cage toward the sharpened silver point that caught the glare of the flashlight beam. One feeble swipe of her arm knocked the flashlight to the ground, sending wicked shadows spinning around her.

The faces of the other girls stared at her from behind their bars, the drugs already taking effect on them. She yelled as he picked the flashlight up and pulled her the rest of the way out of the cage, metal bars scraping hard against her flesh, deep enough to draw blood.

She had time for one final lucid thought, long enough to think "My name is Sue," before the needle pierced her skin, stealing her memories and her will away.

THIRTY-THREE

Logan played a ballad on the piano, humming as Melanie sat at the end of the bench. His voice rose and fell, resting gently on the notes.

"You lied to me," he said, staring at her from beneath a fall of hair across his eyes.

"Lied?" Melanie asked, looking away, studying the wavy shadows the fluorescent lights cast from the soundproofing foam.

"About Casper," he said, returning his fingers to the keys and starting a new song, harder and faster than before. "I saw you two holding hands this morning."

For a long moment, Melanie was silent. "It just sort of happened," she said.

Logan stopped playing long enough to laugh. "Does Daddy know?"

"I thought we were going to practice."

"We are." Logan turned to her, his trademark sneer lifting the corners of his mouth into a parody of a smile. "Did you tell Casper about me?"

"There's nothing to tell."

Logan kept playing with his left hand, picking out half of a song as his right reached out for her, tracing from her cheek to her throat, where the memories of bruises lingered.

Melanie twisted around and stood, heading toward the door. The music grew deeper as Logan's right hand once more joined his left on the keys. "You need to practice to get better," he said as she put her hand on the doorknob.

She looked over her shoulder at him and sighed. "I'll never be better."

Logan stopped playing. "You don't believe that, do you?"

"Doesn't matter what I believe," she said. "It is what it is."

He laughed, then walked to where she stood by the door, her hand still resting on the knob. He placed his palm on her stomach. "From here," he said.

She pushed him away and turned the knob.

"What if being touched makes you better?" he asked, his voice a hard whisper against her skin. "What if giving yourself to me makes you better? Something has to. Let it be me, Melanie."

She studied the room, watching the shadows and the light and the piano, looking everywhere but at Logan.

Once more, he reached out, sliding his hand to rest between her breasts. "Let me help you," he whispered, harsh lips trailing kisses over her cheek. "Sing for me."

She blinked and the fluorescent lights sent shadows dancing

around the room. His palm was a heavy weight against her, but it was distant and meaningless as the shadows flowed across the floor, over the wavy foam walls and the white acoustic tiles of the ceiling.

Melanie smiled.

Logan fit his fingers to where the bruises had been.

She stretched her arms out, the sleeves rising just enough to expose her skin. The shadows crawled up her legs, the cold pouring into her, pouring out of her as the blessed scream began deep within.

"Sing," Logan whispered, pressing harder, the clasp of her bra once more digging into her chest.

Melanie rested her hand on his cheek, sliding an icicle touch down his neck to rest at the base of his throat.

And then she squeezed.

Spinning around, she pushed him against the wall, lifting until his feet no longer touched the ground. With a chorus of shadows inside her, she leaned closer.

Her voice was nothing but the shadow of a whisper. "Never touch me again."

With a shiver, she let go, dropping Logan to the floor. He took gasping gulps of air, coughing as he slowly sat up. She ignored him, listening to the shadows within, desperately hoping to understand. But there was nothing more than a constant, echoing cry.

"Use that," Logan said, coughing out the words. "Whatever the hell that was. Sing, now."

Melanie closed her eyes, stretching her arms out to the

shadows dancing around her, embracing the blizzard within, and sang.

Symphonies of shadows, choruses of angels—Melanie released the building scream. The window in the door shivered, vibrating as each note echoed and soared until the pane shattered, showering the floor with shards of glass.

The song came so naturally; the shadow's true voice finally heard.

She sang.

And it was glorious.

In the corner of the room, Logan watched with his mouth hanging open.

Melanie sang. The music broke free, escaping the room through the broken window. In the hall, students and teachers stopped to listen. The notes reverberated through the building, crystalline and pure, higher and deeper and richer and sacred.

She sang, ethereal and astonishing and beautiful beyond words, turning the plain brick building into her very own cathedral. The passion of the shadows surged through her, driving her onward, rejoicing in song. She sang, and the echoes of her voice wandered the hallways as a sanctified hush filled the school.

———

The constant din of hundreds of students fell silent and I looked up, trying to figure out what had caught everyone's attention, and then I heard it. I heard her. I heard the shadows roaring in her song. I heard Melanie. My chair fell to the ground when I stood, pushing people out of the way in my rush to follow the music.

No one moved around me, heads cocked to the side to hear better. She sang, the song angelic and divine. Notes crawled over each other as though a chorus of thousands had joined together in prayer. But I knew, before I ever reached her side, that Melanie was the only person singing.

I ran through quiet hallways, past silent students and captivated teachers, crying and smiling and listening. Finally I was there, peeking in through the broken window at the glass scattered through the room, at Logan shivering in the corner.

In the middle of the room, Melanie sang with her arms stretched out wide. Shadows flowed across her, in and out of her open mouth, writhing and dancing around her. When our eyes met she sang more brightly still, reaching impossible notes and infinite harmony.

When I reached her side, her skin was pure ice, and steam filled the room the moment we touched. She sang in my embrace, her arms wrapping around me so tightly, so desperately, her singing delicate like the sweetest whisper as the song ended in the rhythm of our kiss.

One student somewhere far away clapped, and the applause built until it seemed as though it would shake the entire school.

In the corner, Logan clapped as well. "That was..." His voice was tinged with something close to awe. "That was everything."

"Melanie," I said, caressing her wintry skin.

She smiled, kissing me one more time. "Everything," she said, and then the shadows flowed into me with a tender, gentle sigh and Melanie collapsed in my arms.

THIRTY-FOUR

She felt so slight when I picked her up, to carry her over the broken glass and out the broken door. I walked through the halls until we reached my car, then slid her into the front seat.

The streets were quiet in the middle of the day, and the drive didn't take very long. I'd thought of heading home, but it was too beautiful a day to be inside. Instead of going to a park, though, I drove to Bonaventure Cemetery. I parked the car and gathered her in my arms again, walking the shaded paths in the cool autumn breeze until we reached her grave.

I sank to the ground, laying her next to me in the grass and running my hands through her hair.

"Melanie," I whispered, again and again. Spanish moss sent dancing shadows around us and I placed a quick kiss on her too-cool skin. At my touch, her eyes opened.

"Hi," she said.

"Good morning."

Melanie smiled, her face lost in the shadows. "She's kissing me." Her fingers caressed her own lips. "And you," she said, before adding her lips to the kiss of the shadow.

For the longest time the only sound was the sigh of the wind though the trees, the beating of my heart keeping time with Melanie's, and the gentle, tender melody of our kiss, joining fire and ice between us.

"I could get used to this," she said.

"Me too." I laughed, the sound so out of place in the cemetery and yet so perfectly at home. "We have a lot of time to make up for, you know."

Melanie smiled, matching my laugh. "I know."

"So," I said, tracing a soft pattern along the curve of her lips, "what do you remember?"

She placed a kiss on my fingertip before turning to study the branches above us. "I told Logan about us," she said. "Melanie was there, everywhere I looked, and I got mad at him. It was strange, how mad I got." She turned to me. "I never get mad; maybe that's part of why I wasn't really able to sing. But I got mad today. Then the shadows were inside me and I was choking Logan, and I guess I understand now what happened when you tried to kill me."

"I'm still sorry about that."

"I know," she said. "When I let him go, he stared at me like I'd lost my mind. Which, come to think of it, I probably have." She laughed, bright and sweet and gone as quickly as it arrived. "Then he told me to sing. So I sang."

"And?" I asked, taking her hand in my own.

"And Melanie was screaming inside me. I heard her adding

her voice to mine. Then I felt all these other voices and it was impossible to stop singing." She shivered as a breeze blew past, sending her hair swirling around us. "It was terrifying and absolutely wonderful."

"Yes," I said. "It was."

"It was so different. I felt different with her inside me," she said. "You paint differently when she's with you, don't you?"

I nodded as shadows danced over my arms, trailing across my lips.

"And then I woke up here, with you." She smiled, leaning in for another eternal kiss. "Aren't we going to get in trouble for leaving school?"

"Probably," I said. "I'm sort of used to it by now."

She laughed, curling into me, and I wrapped my arms around her. "We have to stop meeting like this."

"Fine," I said, squeezing her tighter. "Tomorrow we'll stay in school. Just try not to break any more windows or pass out, okay?"

"Deal."

For a while we just watched the shadows dancing around the cemetery, listening to the breeze whistling through the trees.

"I broke a window?" she asked.

"More like shattered. Least I think it was you," I said. "There was glass everywhere."

"I don't remember that part." She turned around to climb into my lap, straddling my legs and wrapping her arms around me. "Think they'll charge me?"

I smiled, luxuriating in the feel of her in my embrace as the shadows twirled and twisted around us.

"She seems so happy here," Melanie said, resting her head against my shoulder and staring at the shadows with me.

"We've spent a lot of time here," I said. "I would draw, or just sit and talk to you, my eyes closed, pretending you were hiding and listening to me."

"I was always listening to you." She kissed me, so very tenderly. "I talked to you, too," she said. "Not out loud. I didn't want anyone to know. I wanted everyone to think I was normal, that I was fine. But inside, you were always there." She reached out, bringing my fingers to rest above her heart. "You were always here."

I felt the steady pulse beneath my palm, but it was nothing next to feeling the subtle curve of her breast through her shirt. She smiled as my thumb twitched, sliding farther along the lace edge of her bra. Then the shadows were everywhere as her lips met mine, as my hand encompassed her breast. Steam billowed out around us until we were lost in our own private world.

She writhed against me as I pulled her deeper into the kiss. She shivered. She sighed. And then she smiled, breaking the kiss as my hands slid free.

For a moment the only sounds were her short, gasping breaths as she tightened her arms around me. "Yes," she whispered against my neck. "I could get used to that."

Her laugh filled the cemetery as the shadows danced on her grave to the music of her laughter. And gently, tenderly, Melanie sang once more.

THIRTY-FIVE

When we got to my house, we walked inside holding hands and my mom followed us into my room, keeping the door open behind her.

"Detective McGuire called for you. Said to call his cell when you have a moment." As she turned around to leave, she stopped with her hand on the doorknob. "This door stays open." She smiled but didn't move. "Is that understood, you two?"

"Yes, Mrs. Harrison," Melanie said before giving my mom a hug.

"I'm glad you're back," my mom said. "We all are. But you're teenagers, and, well, the door stays open."

"Yes, Mom," I said in my best "I'm fine, yes, Mom" voice, but she wasn't paying much attention to me.

"Want something to drink?" she asked Melanie, and at her nod the two of them left me alone with my phone.

"McGuire," he said, answering on the third ring.

"Hi, it's Richard Harrison. My mom said you called." I fell into my desk chair, spinning it around to rest my elbows on the desk.

"I wanted to see if you were doing okay."

"I'm fine, thanks." I took a deep breath, letting it out in a rush. "Anything new?"

"Not much I can share with you," he said. "But I wanted to tell you there's going to be a report released soon. That's why I called. We kept your name out of it. Didn't see anything to be gained by naming you."

"Thanks," I said. "I guess I hadn't thought about it."

"You'd have had the media camping out on your street, asking a thousand questions you wouldn't have wanted to answer." I heard his pen tapping on the metal desk, a steady clicking sound. "Instead I get to answer all of them. But I get paid for the privilege."

"Thanks, again," I said, not sure what else to say.

"I also thought you'd want to know we're all finished out on the island. The clearing's sort of back to what it was. Wasn't sure if you'd want to paint there anymore or not, but I figured you deserved to know you can. Anyway, you have my number if you think of anything else, Richard," he said. "Okay?"

And then he was gone and I was alone, the shadows still and silent. I opened a local news website and there it was, the top story. A mass grave found near Fort McAllister. Fourteen skeletons. Fourteen names beneath fourteen photographs. Fourteen missing girls from around the United States, identified by DNA.

And not one single girl named Melanie Elizabeth Bellemeade.

The shadow clawed her way out of me, roaring louder than I'd ever heard her, ripping my own cry out of me. In a heartbeat Melanie and my mother were there, speaking to me, but the screams drowned out their voices. Melanie's arms were ice as they wrapped around me, enveloping me in the winter of her.

"Richard, what happened?" Her dark, dark eyes opened wide, her skin freezing as I rested my over-heated palms on her skin.

"Richard?" my mother asked.

"It's okay," I said, even though it wasn't. "Just been that kind of day."

"What kind of day?" she asked, turning to Melanie for an answer.

"The screaming kind," I said, attempting to joke and failing miserably.

"Have you been taking your pills?"

"Every day," I said, even though I didn't think they did anything. "Can I have some water, please?" I added, simply to get her out of the room.

She nodded before leaving Melanie and me alone.

"What happened?" Melanie asked again, her voice low.

"That," I said, pointing at the monitor.

Fourteen young girls, smiling in school portraits or casual birthday party photographs, most of them black and white. All of those lonely skeletons found by me, on Savage Island.

"Wait," she said, resting her fingers on the screen. "Where's Melanie?"

I shrugged, the shadows thundering still. "I don't know," I said. "I just don't know."

After my mother brought me water, she left us alone, and Melanie and I read through the other news reports. Nothing was different in any of them. There were a total of fourteen skeletons, and all fourteen had been identified. Parents from across the country were flying to Savannah to claim their missing daughters and have some semblance of closure.

"Ask her," Melanie said.

"Who?"

"Melanie," she said. "If she's inside me, ask her. She's sort of spoken to you before."

I kissed her, a brush of my lips against her skin, trailing a slow line of kisses up to her ear. "Melanie," I said, nothing but a soft breath of air.

"Still me," she said with a sigh. "I can hear her, though, if that helps."

"Maybe we need a Ouija board."

She rolled her eyes and laughed. "Just try again."

"Melanie," I said, "please, talk to me."

Dark shadows danced along my arm, followed by Melanie's finger tracing the same path, the raw touch of ice numbing my skin.

"Please," I said again. "Tell me what happened to you."

The shadow reached the sleeve of my shirt and stopped, drawing a line around my biceps until Melanie pulled the shirt over my head. The shadows exploded across my bare skin, Melanie's arms wrapping around me.

I counted to one hundred. I counted again, the silence all consuming, waiting, praying for an answer.

"I can feel his hands," she replied at last, a thousand voices whispering, echoing in symphony. "I can feel them, around my neck."

I was afraid to breathe, afraid to move. Against my back, Melanie's hands curled into fists, digging her nails into my flesh, drawing frigid lines of ice.

"We're not alone," she said, another thousand voices adding to the chorus.

Melanie stabbed her nails into my back and I felt blood slipping down my skin like tears.

"There's someone watching us, watching him kill me. Watching me die," she whispered in a chorus of voices, and then the multitude was gone and her eyes were just dark blue again.

For a long moment neither of us moved, my skin stinging where Melanie had ripped it open, her tears wet on my shoulder as we held onto each other for support.

"This is why I want the door open," my mother said, walking into the room.

"Nothing happened," I said, my voice rougher than I intended.

"My fault," Melanie said. "I was crying on his shoulder and his shirt got all wet."

My mom went in a drawer and tossed me another shirt. I kept my back to the wall until I was able to pull the new shirt on.

"I should get going," Melanie said. "Can you take me to my car? It's still at school."

I nodded and we left my mom in my room.

"Hold on a second." I ran back to where my mom was still staring at the fourteen pictures on the monitor. "Really, Mom, nothing happened."

"I know."

"Not after that," I said, pointing at the screen.

She kissed my cheek. "Are you okay?" she asked as we headed to the front door where Melanie was waiting for us.

"I'm okay."

"Be good to her," my mother said.

"Yeah," Melanie said as we drove away, taking my hand and holding on tightly. "Be good to me."

THIRTY-SIX

When I entered the performing arts wing the next day, there was a big piece of cardboard duct-taped over the broken window. The door was open and Melanie was sitting on the piano bench, idly running her hands across the keys and humming quietly to herself.

"Hi," I said, leaning against the wall.

She tilted her head and smiled at me. Her hair curled around her neck, sparkling with copper embers in the harsh fluorescent light. My breath caught when she licked her lips, the shine of them brighter now. For a brief instant, she bit her bottom lip and I lost most of the feeling in my legs.

"It's different," she said, breaking off the song. "Singing without her. It sounds wrong. I know the notes aren't flat, but the singing is, which probably doesn't make much sense."

"I know," I said, moving to sit next to her on the bench.

"I have hundreds of drawings I've done with her, and almost as many I did without. You can compare them, if you're bored and have nothing better to do with your life."

She laughed. "Okay," she said.

"Flat is a good word for it," I said. "For the ones I did by myself. The word works for paintings, too."

"What do you think happened?" she asked. "To her?"

I placed my hand on the keys and did the only thing I'd ever learned to do with a piano—poke the same key again and again until I grew bored and moved to the next key, then do the same thing there.

Melanie slammed her hand onto my finger. "No more," she said with a smile. "That's beyond annoying."

"I know," I said. "Isn't it wonderful?"

She rested her head on my shoulder, pillowed by her hair, and merged her fingers with mine. "Yes," she said. "Wonderful."

"I don't know," I said. "About what happened to her. She led me to those bones—maybe she was there once?"

"Someone moved her?"

"She said someone watched him kill her. So maybe there were two people?"

"Doesn't help much."

"No." I turned to her, resting my forehead on hers. "Nothing helps. I figured they'd identify her and, well, after that she'd be at peace or something."

"You thought she'd leave you, didn't you? That's why you didn't want to go to the police." She kissed me for a moment as the shadows flowed around the room.

"Us," I said, breaking her kiss. "She'll leave us."

"She's here," Melanie said with a smile. "I can see her."

"I know."

"I think she likes it when we kiss," Melanie said, brushing her polar lips over my skin.

"And sing," I said.

"And paint."

"But mostly this," I said, placing my flaming hands on her frosty cheeks and drawing her into a steaming kiss.

———

In the cafeteria, Max walked to the table carrying two trays, Caitlin trailing behind. Her hair was tied in a swirling bun, stray strands of blonde hair curling around her face, framing her smile. Her bright green eyes sparkled at Max as he put her tray down, pulled out her seat, and sat next to her.

"Well," I said. "What's new?"

Max smiled. "Nothing," he said, "nothing at all." And then he reached out and took Caitlin's hand in his. "Why? What's new with you?"

"Oh, fine," Melanie said, reaching for my hand. "Are we going to double date now?"

"No," Max, Caitlin, and I said at the same time.

"Why not?" Melanie asked. "It'd be fun."

"Your dad, for one thing," I said.

"There's a group of us," she said with a wicked little smile. "That's allowed."

I matched her smile. "Double date it is."

"Do I have a say in this?" Max asked.

"No," Caitlin, Melanie, and I said at the same time.

Logan passed by, nodding to us on the way to his own table. His blank stare beneath his all-American hair was different somehow, as though he was finally paying attention to other human beings. Melanie waved but didn't let go of my hand.

"He said you passed out," Caitlin said, looking at us. It was going to take a very long time to get used to seeing her face when she spoke. Before today, I wasn't sure I'd ever seen all of it at once.

"Long story," Melanie said. "But I'm fine."

"Everyone heard you singing," Max said. "They're still talking about the broken window."

A blush spread over Melanie's skin. "I didn't mean to do that."

"It is pretty cool," I said.

"Now they'll never let me sing again."

"Not around glass, at least," Max said.

He and Caitlin walked off holding hands, Caitlin brushing against Max's shoulder. At the table, Melanie sighed. "Doesn't matter," she said, barely speaking out loud.

"What doesn't?" I asked.

"The singing." She closed her eyes, resting her chin in her palms. "She won't be with me for every performance. That's no way to live, is it? I can't sing without her."

"Yes," I said, resting my hand on her shoulder, feeling the subtle sobs shuddering through her. "You can. I heard you."

"You heard *her*," Melanie said with another shiver.

"No." I pressed a kiss against her forehead. "Sure, I heard her too." She looked at me, her red eyes blinking tears. "You were both singing, yes, but it was your voice."

"So," she said, "do you mean you're okay with her leaving and you being just an ordinary artist?"

It was impossible to process the idea of my life without the shadow in it. The emptiness that had engulfed me when Melanie first disappeared returned, threatening to swallow me completely. I took a deep breath, and another, as Melanie shivered against me.

"Will you be there with me?" I asked finally, caressing a tear off her cheek and casting a shadow on her lips.

Melanie's smile was soft and sweet and glorious.

The shadows were calm and warm, gentle and tender. Somewhere in the echoes an apology lingered, along with just a subtle breath of jealousy as Melanie kissed me.

"Still afraid she'll leave you?" Melanie asked, breaking the kiss only when a teacher wandered by and knocked on the table.

I nodded, and the shadow exploded to life. "Yes," I said, forcing the word out through clenched teeth. "But she's earned her rest—she deserves to be at peace. I can't keep that from her just because I'll miss her."

Melanie smiled, stroking icy fingers over my skin. "So warm," she said with a smile. "What now?"

"I've been thinking we should go to Dublin," I said. "Most of the local reports from 1997 aren't online. The Laurens County Library has them in archives. Maybe that'll help?"

"Can't hurt, can it?" Melanie asked. "It's not like her bones were found and the police are looking into it."

"I know," I said. "I just feel like the right thing to do is to help her find her way home."

"I'm going to miss her too, you know," Melanie said, her smile sad and beautiful.

"Thanks," I said.

"For what?"

"Everything."

"Everything is just beginning," she said, kissing me one more time, the shadow piercing us both.

THIRTY-SEVEN

After school, I sat at home waiting for Melanie to call so we could take I-16 to Dublin, but by the time she called I'd run into one small problem. The Neon decided it had no interest in driving any farther. None at all. It didn't even want to drive to Melanie's house, since we'd planned on taking her car. Sure, the old car sounded as though it was trying, but it was only mocking me.

My mother, always helpful, called a friend who fixed cars before I even had a chance to call Melanie to come get me. By the time I talked to her, it was later than we'd wanted to leave.

"We can go tomorrow," I said, hoping to keep the frustration out of my voice.

"My dad's off tomorrow," she said. "It's okay. Wait for the mechanic. I'll drive up by myself and go to the library, make copies of everything."

The shadow stalked the street, circling the car as I leaned on the hood and talked to Melanie.

"I've got directions," she said with a laugh. "Besides, I like road trips."

"No speeding."

"I know," she said, and then she was gone and the shadow and I were alone in the middle of the street, kicking the uncaring tires of my car.

———————

The GPS directed Melanie west out of Savannah. After a little less than two hours of driving, she reached the brick building on Elm Street in the small town of Dublin, Georgia. After she parked, she called Richard.

"I'm here," she said.

"And I'm still here, waiting on this guy who was supposed to be here a while ago."

She laughed, then said goodbye before entering the building.

At the front desk, a young man with a scruffy beard and a nametag that identified him as the librarian was playing a game on his phone. He glanced at Melanie and slid his glasses off. "May I help you?"

"I hope so," she said. "I'm looking for archives from the *Courier-Herald*, around 1997."

"The archives are downstairs," he said, leading her to the elevator. "Anything in particular you're interested in?"

"It's a school assignment," she said. "We're supposed to

research our names, and I ran across references to a missing girl. Just sort of wondering if they ever found her, I guess. Couldn't find anything online."

"Aren't too many missing kids around here," he said. "Of course, I lived in Madison back in '97, so I wasn't paying much attention."

In the archives room, the librarian turned on a microfiche machine, ran through the instructions, and left her with the films.

Melanie rushed by reports on local court cases and the occasional tornado before reaching the handful of articles on Melanie Elizabeth Bellemeade. Ignoring the signs about not using a cell phone, she photographed each article as it appeared, sending the pictures to Richard.

After the second picture, her phone rang.

"Thanks," he said.

"Figured you'd appreciate it."

"Mechanic's here. I appreciate that." He laughed, but it didn't last long. "Find anything else?"

Sitting in front of the machine, Melanie shrugged. "Not much. Most of this is just background information. Her mom and stuff. There's a little bit here about Stephen Bellemeade, her father. It was a messy divorce, so the police tracked him down out in Nevada. Anyway, they cleared him and pretty much never mention him again."

"Well, I guess that's something, at least."

"At the very least," she said. "Did you know she had a brother?"

"No," he said. "Older or younger?"

"Younger, I think." Melanie scrolled to the last article she'd found. "Seems to have been born a little after Melanie disappeared; they don't mention him much, not even a name." She scanned through the short article. "That's it. Nothing else."

"Hold on a second," Richard said. "The mechanic's waving. Let me call you back."

Moving forward in time on the machine, Melanie searched the *Courier-Herald* archives for 1998 and 1999, looking for some closure or follow-up. Unfortunately, there was nothing beyond a brief mention on the one-year anniversary, basically informing the world that Melanie Elizabeth Bellemeade had still not been found. The short article was achingly depressing in its banality and lack of information.

In the car, Melanie turned the heat on and then called Richard.

"I'm all done," she said.

"Me too," Richard said. "The guy just left. Cost my parents a couple hundred, but the car's working again."

"That's good, right?"

"Right."

"The *Courier-Herald* really didn't have very much," she said. "The only thing I learned was that as of 1999, her mom still lived in the same house outside of Dublin. Nothing very helpful, though."

"And her dad?"

"Still out in Nevada, as far as I could tell. Should be in the fourth picture I sent you."

"Thanks," he said. "Are you driving back now?"

For a long moment Melanie just stared out the window, at the shadows thrown by the trees surrounding the library. In the wind, the branches stirred just enough to send them flickering all around her. She shook her head even though he couldn't see her. "No," she said. "I think I'm going to drive out to Melanie's old house. I just want to see it, see where she grew up. Does that make sense? Who knows, maybe her mom still lives there."

"Yeah," he said. "Maybe. Take some pictures for me, please."

By the time Melanie reached Claxton Dairy Road, the sun was approaching the horizon. It was a quiet, simple house, with a broken rocking chair on a wrap-around porch; almost inviting despite the slightly run-down nature of everything. The paint was peeling off the steps, even though it looked as if it had once been lovingly painted a bright, cheerful color that had faded, like the house itself, over the years. *Probably since their daughter went missing*, Melanie thought. The entire home seemed to be in mourning, still breathing but not truly living.

She snapped a couple of pictures and texted them to Richard with the address, before deciding to knock on the door and maybe meet Melanie's mother.

THIRTY-EIGHT

Melanie took her time walking on the cracked sidewalk, looking up and down the street. The other houses were few and far between and seemed uninhabited; everything was deserted and neglected. At the door, she hesitated for a long moment before knocking, ignoring the *No Solicitation* sign that had also faded with time. Through the window, she saw a wall of photographs stretching floor to ceiling, watching over the living room. She shivered once as a cold breeze blew past, and then knocked again, the deep hollow thuds the only sound.

She heard footsteps and creaking floorboards behind the door, and then it opened with a squeal of rusty hinges. A woman stood there in blue jeans and a misbuttoned flannel shirt, her graying hair wet as though she'd just jumped out of the shower.

"I'm sorry," Melanie said. "I didn't mean to interrupt anything."

"No problem," the woman said. "I didn't need to waste all that water anyway. Can I help you with something?"

"Melanie," she said, introducing herself. "Melanie Robins. I'm doing this all wrong." She squeezed her hands together, staring into the woman's lined face, which looked as though it had been in a perpetual frown for a very long time.

"Where are my manners," the woman said, a sudden smile transforming her, making her appear years younger. "Please come in."

Melanie took a deep breath and crossed the threshold. A single lamp lit the room with yellowish light, shining on the hundreds of framed and unframed pictures covering the living room walls. The dilapidated furniture was as yellow as the light, the faded patterns hidden behind layers of dust. Melanie followed the woman to the kitchen, relishing its bright, fluorescent light after the darkness in the rest of the house.

In the kitchen, the walls were covered with even more photographs. A smiling young girl, no more than six or seven, was in every single one of them. School portraits, casual family photos... thousands of pictures of Melanie Elizabeth Bellemeade wallpapering the walls.

"My daughter," the woman said, pointing toward the pictures. "Her name was Melanie, too."

"I know," Melanie said, turning in a slow circle to see all of them. "That's why I'm here. I'm new in town and was doing some research for a school project, and—" Her voice ran dry as the woman stared at her. She swallowed. "And I wanted to meet you, I guess. I'm sorry for your loss, I mean. And for bothering you. I should have called first."

"Nonsense," the woman said. "I'm glad you're here. I don't get to talk about my Melanie enough. No one wants to listen to an old woman rambling, you know?"

"I don't mind."

"It's Jessica, by the way," she said. "Jessica Bellemeade. It's been a long time since I've had any real company, Melanie. So, tell me, what type of research are you doing?"

"Supposed to be a history lesson on our names," she said. "I started researching 'Melanie' and, well, here I am. I guess I just wanted to know if Melanie was ever found."

Jessica shook her head, her shoulders slumped. "No," she said, a faint tremor in the single word. "She was never found." With a sigh she crossed the kitchen to the stove. "Tea?" she asked, and at Melanie's nod she turned the stove on, blue flames crackling to life.

———

After reading through all the articles and staring at the pictures of the old house Melanie had sent me, I called her, but only her voicemail answered. As she'd said, there wasn't much new information in the archived reports; nothing I didn't already know, for the most part. I called her phone a second time, but there was still no answer.

———

Jessica was silent for a long moment until she picked up the whistling teakettle and carried it to the counter, taking two cups off a shelf. "It's my own blend," she said. "One of the benefits of owning a farm, even if I'm no longer a farmer. Least not since my husband left." She brought a tray to the table, complete with cubes of sugar. "Please, Melanie, sit."

"Thanks."

"Try it with two cubes," Jessica said, sliding into the seat across from Melanie. "That's the way I like it."

As Jessica stirred her own tea, she kept staring at the pictures on the wall. "I loved her very much," she said. "She was an amazing little girl. Always full of laughter. It filled the house." She looked at the ceiling, her eyes misting. "There hasn't been laughter in this place for a very long time now." She was silent for a long while, and then turned to Melanie. "How's your tea?"

"It's good," Melanie said after taking a sip. "Sweet."

Jessica smiled, the frown lines fading. "You might have only needed one cube then, I guess." She stirred her tea some more, turning to the photos of her daughter. "Her dad used to pretend he was a photographer; always had a camera in his hands. Every time Melanie smiled, he'd take another picture."

Melanie put her empty china cup on the matching china saucer.

"All finished with your tea, dear?" Jessica asked.

Melanie nodded. "Yes," she said. "I wouldn't mind another cup, if you have more."

Jessica smiled again. "Oh, I don't think that would be the best idea," she said, taking Melanie's empty cup and her own full one to the sink and dumping her untouched tea down the drain. When she turned around, her smile was far away and forgotten. "You look tired, Melanie. Perhaps you'd like to lie down and take a nap before driving home?"

Melanie turned to her, but the motion never stopped, as though she were watching the world through a panoramic lens. The whole room seemed to float from side to side. Her head flopped onto her shoulders.

"Maybe you should rest for just a little bit," Jessica said. She came around the table to tug on Melanie's shoulder until Melanie dragged herself up and followed her to the living room, shuffling her feet across the hard wooden floors, kicking up dust with each step.

"Here you go." Jessica helped her lie on the dusty couch, the countless photos of a smiling little girl following her every move. "You look just like her, you know, dear," Jessica said, running her fingers through Melanie's hair.

"Your daughter?" Melanie managed to ask, the words slurred and slow. She tried to focus on the words, or the pictures on the wall, or on standing up and walking to her car and driving home, but nothing worked quite right.

Jessica laughed, a light distant sort of laugh. "No, sweetheart," she said, "of course not. You look just like your mother."

THIRTY-NINE

She struggled to open her eyes, the lids so heavy. Far too heavy. Heavy and weighted down with something damp, something that smelled overwhelmingly foul. Smelled of sweat and something spoiled and rotten and something else she couldn't name. Didn't want to name.

She struggled to remember her name. It was there, somewhere. Somewhere deep inside. But all the thoughts and all the names and all the words were floating, sliding as she reached for them in the darkness. There was nothing but those heavy lids and the dampness pressing on them and the darkness and the floating thoughts. Floating free.

She struggled to move, but nothing worked, nothing moved. A finger, just a finger. Twitch, please, just for a moment, an instant, anything, anywhere. But nothing moved. So heavy. Damp. She strained to open her eyes, to remember her name, to move, but there was nothing.

Nowhere. Her tongue rested heavily against her teeth, tasting of metal and fabric. Every breath filled her lungs with stale air, old and overused.

"Melanie." A voice spoke somewhere in the darkness, somewhere in the depths of the shadows. It might have been a word, might have been a name. The voice was soft and hard and far away and far too close and there was nothing but the word and the word was meaningless.

After grabbing a quick dinner, I called Melanie again, listening to her voicemail, leaving increasingly worried messages. The shadow howled, frantic, anxious, and desperate as I looked at the blurry photos of her old house.

After leaving one final message I gave up, jumped in the car, and took off, forcing the Neon faster and faster as we sped west on 16.

The blindfold was ripped off and she blinked against the sudden brightness, nothing in focus beyond the length of her arm. Her head rested on her shoulder and she tried to see her hand, unmoving where a rope wrapped around it, hanging from the ceiling. She fought to look to the other side but merely managed to catch a glimpse, her head crashing to her chest, where more ropes circled her. Her entire body was suspended from the ceiling, her feet swinging above the floor.

The voice came again, a distant, echoing, feminine whisper. "The drugs should be wearing off soon, dear."

Melanie blinked, fighting to move her tongue enough to speak, but no sound emerged.

"I have a present for you, Melanie," Jessica said, walking into the shadows of the room. "All these years, I saved it just for you."

Melanie tried to see through the drugs and the gloom, but the light didn't penetrate very far. A rough scratching sound echoed all around her, like something heavy being dragged, and then Jessica reappeared, humming a half-forgotten lullaby while pulling a long flat trunk across the floor.

Even through the drugs, Melanie raged within as she stared at her box.

"You have to understand," Jessica said, her voice little more than a crackle of sound. "I knew all his secrets, but after you disappeared, he changed. Thought he was in love with her again."

"You knew my mother?" Melanie asked, the words barely understandable, letters slurring into each other.

"Of course, dear," she said. "Though I only met her the one time. The day she died." A burst of brittle laughter shot through the room, echoing in the shadows. "It took me years to find them again. To find him."

"Who?" Melanie asked, the word yelled out into the darkness so forcefully it set her swinging from the ceiling, the ropes squealing through the pulleys.

"Our husband, of course," she said. "Well, not really. She never knew, the foolish girl, trying to take him from me.

There was so much she never knew about your father, about all his toys out on that island. But I knew everything. I knew you were his favorite. I knew what he was saving you for."

———————

It took far too long to reach Dublin. The sun had already set as I wandered past all the rural farms searching for Claxton Dairy Road. When I arrived at the Bellemeade house, one lonely light was on. I climbed the porch stairs and banged on the front door. The shadow twisted and writhed around me in a frenzy of activity, never stopping to rest for more than a moment.

But no matter how hard I banged, there was no answer.

———————

For a moment, no longer, Melanie looked up, just as her body swung around. A small round table set for tea flickered out of the shadows, and, beyond, rows of animal cages were stacked on top of each other. Five lonely, frightened pairs of eyes were watching her swing. And then the ropes twisted her around and the image sank into the shadows.

Jessica approached Melanie, grabbing her hair to pull her close. "Melanie walked in on him," she said, the words hissed out. "Playing with one of his toys. She'd been trained better than to make too much noise, but she did anyway. She screamed when he wouldn't let her play with the little girl too. She'd still be alive if she'd ever just learned how to be quiet. To keep her mouth shut. To leave him alone when he was playing. He always liked it quiet, you know?"

Jessica twirled Melanie around as though they were dancing. The ropes tightened on her wrists with a metallic squeal, pulling her farther from the floor. She yelled, a harsh sound ripped from her throat.

"It was all her fault," Jessica said. "She left him no choice. He killed my daughter, my Melanie. He made me watch. He smiled at me as she turned blue." A cruel laugh burst forth again. "So I killed his wife. I made him watch as she turned red."

Jessica's laughter echoed through the shadows. From the cages surrounding them, frightened voices cried out in answer.

"He even named you Melanie for me," she said. "Because I asked him to, because I threatened to take you away from him if he didn't. He was always so nice to me, took care of me. He would take me to the island, to Melanie's grave, and hold my hand while I cried." She sniffled, wiping her eyes. She studied the tears and then licked her hands clean. "And then he moved back here, with you, and he didn't come for me. He left me here. He kept you all to himself. He wouldn't tell me where you were. I had to find other Melanies. But there was always something wrong with them. They never worked quite right. And now you're here, another Melanie, just for me."

Melanie screamed as the ropes twisted and twirled. She turned around and turned around, but there was no one there, no one but five terrified girls in their dirty cages, watching her with horrified eyes.

I took my phone out, dialed, and once more listened to it ring, and then listened to Melanie's voice asking if I wanted to leave a message. I was about to give up on anyone answering the door and just head back to the car to drive around Dublin searching for her, but I knocked one final time. A harried voice spoke from the other side.

"Just a moment," a woman said, opening the door just wide enough to peek through.

I could barely see the gray hair and the piercing black eye staring at me, but it was enough. The shadow flew through the opening, spreading out to explore the house. Even from so far away, I heard the shadow's anger and frustration at not finding Melanie inside.

"May I help you?" the woman said, still not opening the door.

But she didn't need to. I already knew Melanie wasn't there.

"Hi," I said, holding my arm out for the shadow to crawl across my skin. "A friend of mine said she might stop here for a school project, and since she's not answering her phone, I figured I'd drive by."

"Oh," she said, "no, I'm sorry, there's no one here but me." She opened the door wider. "You're welcome to come in. I just put on a pot of tea, if you'd like."

"That's okay, thanks," I said, anxious to return to the car and continue my search.

The woman stood in her doorway, casting a long shadow

on the porch as I walked away. I waved before putting the car into drive.

The shadow was an inferno, roaring far too loudly for me to see straight, and I slammed on the brakes before I'd even reached the stop sign at the end of the road.

I rested my forehead on the steering wheel and once more dialed Melanie's phone, listened to the same message, her voice filling the car. Everything burned so brightly, blinding me, deafening me. And then the shadow dropped to silence and only my left arm burned, the heat rising until it moved, all on its own, to rest on the door handle.

After getting out, I stood in darkness on the side of the road. Then the shadow led me through the woods surrounding the Bellemeade farm as though she'd lived there all of her life. Which, I guess, she had.

Step by step, the shadow and I crossed unused, wild fields overgrown with weeds to a small barn far behind the main house. The red paint had long since faded to pink, and in the pale moonlight the wood boarding all the windows blended into the same color.

I walked as quietly as possible, rising on tiptoes to try to see inside, peeking between the boards over the closest window, but there was nothing to see, no light reaching inside.

I had just opened the flashlight app on my phone when something cold and metallic pressed against my neck, pinning me against the faded pink barn.

"You shouldn't be here," a male voice said, taking my phone and then grabbing me by the scruff of my neck. He kept the barrel of the gun against my shoulder as he pushed me forward into the barn. A single light illuminated Melanie—hanging from the ceiling, crucified by the ropes hanging around her.

For a moment, an instant, she looked up as I called her name, but I didn't think she was able to see me in the shadows. Then the barrel of the gun landed on the side of my head with a thunderous echo and I couldn't breathe, couldn't move, couldn't think. Everything went black and everything changed and everything disappeared, and all I knew was pain. Unending, unceasing pain.

FORTY

I struggled to open my eyes, the lids so heavy. Far too heavy. Nothing worked right and tightness radiated in waves from the base of my skull. Beneath my cheek, the hard wood floor stabbed splinters into my skin and I blinked against the light. Everything was sideways, tilting, falling. I tried to push myself up, but my hands wouldn't move; something was tightly binding them together, cutting off the circulation.

There was a shout, somewhere far too close, and I blinked at the sound. Shadows surrounded me, but pain muted their screams, drained their heat. At the edge of my vision, a wall of metal bars hovered above me, looking like they were about to fall and crush me. From between the closest bars, a pale, small arm extended almost far enough to reach me, one thin finger pointing to the other side of the room.

Frightened eyes peered out of the shadows behind the bars, staring past me. I took as deep a breath as the ropes allowed and flopped my head away from those terrified eyes. The movement hurt beyond words, shooting agony through me, but even the pain was far removed, as though it were happening to someone else.

The room was tilted, my view half blocked by my own hair, as the rest of the barn came into focus. At first it was difficult to tell what I was seeing—the back of a young man, holding a shotgun that was dripping my blood from its barrel. Beyond him, Melanie still hung from ropes in the shadows. The woman I'd just spoken to stood at her feet, holding on to her legs.

"It's going to be all right," Jessica Bellemeade said, her voice humming a wicked lullaby.

The flickering fluorescent bulb hanging next to Melanie sent shadows writhing around the room. Hair hung in thick strands around her motionless face.

The shadow flowed across me. It engulfed my hands, swallowing the ropes, but even though it felt as though I were on fire, nothing happened; the pain was a distant ache, muted and incomplete.

"The drugs are going to wear off soon," the man said.

"You're safe now," she said, brushing her fingers through Melanie's hair. "Everything's okay."

"Mother," he said. "You need to give them more."

"Shhh, child," she said, standing to take Melanie in her arms, the body swinging with a squeal of rusty pulleys. "Mommy's here. I've always been here, watching over you, taking care of you." She pulled Melanie close, wrapping wasted arms around her.

"No," Melanie said, the word ripped out of her throat, echoing through the barn.

Shadows swarmed Jessica and her son, but they paid no attention. No one paid any attention.

Behind me, an anxious cry burst from the cages. More followed, and when I flipped my head I saw thin arms stretching between the bars, reaching out to the ropes tied around my wrists.

With a deep breath, I rolled far enough to slam my back into the bars. Something wet and cold caught on my skin and through the haze of pain I felt fresh blood seeping out of the recently healed scratches Melanie had left.

"I watched over you." Jessica continued her lullaby, adding words to the quiet melody. "Always watching over you. I watched you and that little boy playing hide-and-seek. I watched you run into the woods." She pushed and Melanie went flying through the air, her arms stretched tight, nearly pulled out of their sockets.

"I followed you, brought you home," she said, gray hair swirling around her as the lullaby turned into a curse. "I took care of you. I even cleaned the soda stain off the shirt you were wearing, and all those bloody scratches. So much blood. Then I called that woman, invited her to my house. It was perfect."

"Mother," her son said, reaching out to her. She smacked him, the slap echoing through the barn.

"No!" she shrieked. "No, she never showed up and that other man took you from me. I couldn't tell Daddy. No,

I couldn't tell him. He'd punish me if he knew I'd had his daughter and let her slip away."

The shadows ran across my skin, closer now as the headache and the pain slowly receded. Screams teased at the edge of hearing, the burn at the edge of fire as hands clawed at my wrists, tugging on the ropes.

"He'd have loved me so much if I'd returned you to him," Jessica said, catching Melanie in the middle of her swing and running her hands over Melanie's face. "I saved you, and I couldn't tell him. I didn't dare. He was always being so naughty. Always bringing his problems here for me to take care of. But now you're home, Melanie. Back where you belong."

She turned to her son. "We don't need the others. They never worked right anyway." She turned all her attention to Melanie. "Just this one. Just my daughter, just Melanie. Home at last."

"Mother," he said as he walked to her. "They need more drugs."

Melanie glanced up from beneath the fall of her dirty hair, the shadows crawling over her the way they were crawling over me, the pain almost gone, the shadows almost home.

"Get rid of them," Jessica said, placing a single kiss on Melanie's forehead. "I don't need anyone but my daughter."

"Where?"

"With the others," she said. "I don't care. Just get rid of them."

Her son reached out, placing a hand on her shoulder. "I already told you," he said. "They found the others."

"Help me," Melanie said, her voice a pale imitation of a whisper, but she wasn't looking at me. She was looking at Jessica's son.

In response, he turned from her, turned around, turned toward me. As the light hit him, he smiled, but it was as empty as always beneath his all-American hair.

"I'm trying," Logan answered her, even though he was staring directly at me. "But you shouldn't have come here."

"Shhh, Melanie." Jessica continued to whisper her lullaby but no one was paying attention. "Mommy's here now."

"Please," Melanie whispered, pleading, her voice breaking on the word.

Logan turned to her, moving far enough from his mother to stay out of her reach. "I kept you safe," he said. "I didn't even tell her where you were, that you'd returned to Savannah. Why did you come here? Why did either of you come here?"

"Help me," Melanie said again, before her head dropped, fighting the pull of gravity and losing.

Small fingers scratched at my wrists, frantically trying to loosen the ropes. The heat from the shadow was closer but still so far away as the pain receded and the world slowly came into focus.

"I can't help you," Logan said, reaching out to try to stop Melanie from swinging but only managing to send her spinning in circles.

"She's mine," Jessica said, jumping in front of her son and grabbing onto Melanie, her weight pulling them to a stop. "You can have the other ones."

Logan looked at his mother and grabbed his shotgun.

As the barrel swung around, I wasn't sure who he was planning to shoot. Then he turned to me and smiled that sneer of a smile.

"You were always in the way, Casper," he said as he raised the gun.

The ropes around my wrists fell free. The blood rushed into my fingers, pins and needles pounding into them, but they were free, free and awake. The shadow burst through me like a wave crashing on the shore, filling me with righteous fire and vengeful wrath. I pushed myself up, stumbling once and then staggering forward, barreling into Logan right as he pulled the trigger. The thunder of the shot deafened me and I felt something tear into my shoulder.

The shotgun went flying as I crashed into him. Even though he was bigger than me, it didn't matter. Nothing mattered. Nothing but the need of the shadow to hurt, to kill. The hunger of the flames, the need of the damned for salvation. And deliverance was here.

———————

Steam rose from the ropes bound around Melanie, her dark, dark eyes bright in the shadows. Her body twisted, spinning in the air as the ropes turned to ice, splitting into pieces and falling to the ground like snow. As the drugs faded, the voices of the shadows screamed through her. Melanie cried out as she fell to the floor at Jessica's feet, the ropes nothing but puddles. Everything hurt but the shadow seethed inside, driving her to stand, pushing her forward, pulling her body up, forcing her to move, demanding she move. And Melanie moved. One slow step at a time. She moved.

Jessica kept crooning her lullaby, calling to her lost daughter. The shadows were avenging angels, vengeful spirits raging with sound and fury.

"Melanie," Jessica said. "Mommy's here, you're safe, you're home."

The shadows wrapped long, delicate, almost skeletal fingers around Jessica's neck and squeezed, lifting her off the ground until Melanie's arm pointed straight to heaven, dangling Jessica Bellemeade in the air.

"She's mine," Logan said as he slammed his boot into my side, rocking me with the blow, but the shadows were everywhere, flowing around me, flowing through me, their cries a wordless source of power. I grabbed his legs and he fell across me, his weight driving the air out of my lungs. We rolled across the wood floor of the ancient barn until we came to a stop against the cages.

Thin fingers poked out from between the bars, stabbing into him with ragged fingernails, scratching and tearing, ripping out hair, raking at his skin.

Logan kicked out, knocking me back, and when I landed a sharp stabbing pain shot into my knee from landing on the shotgun. And then he was on top of me again, slamming his fists into my stomach, my chest, my face.

"Melanie," Jessica choked out, struggling for breath, struggling to breathe. "Mommy's here."

Melanie fought the shadow within, fought to find her own voice. "You," she whispered through clenched teeth, battling the blizzard storming through her. "You killed—" The cry thundered louder, raging inside, and still she fought to find herself.

Melanie squeezed more tightly, squeezed and squeezed until the lullaby finally faded away.

"You killed my mother."

The shadow writhed inside, absorbing the blows, igniting within, exploding out of me. Logan twisted, bringing his hands together around my throat. He squeezed. My lungs burned, stars popping in and out of my vision. I didn't know where the shotgun had fallen. I tried to reach for it, but his knees trapped my arms against my sides and I felt weaker every second. The shadow raged, but her precious screams seemed farther and farther from me with every fading beat of my heart.

From somewhere in the darkness, the old woman flew through the air and landed with a thud at the base of the cages. The girls cried out, and for a moment, an instant, a second, Logan paused to watch his mother fly.

It was all I needed.

His weight shifted as she landed against the cages, and the shotgun was in my hand in a heartbeat. The blast echoed for an eternity, deafening, as Logan flew backward to land in a heap next to his mother.

Melanie collapsed against me, bleeding from countless cuts. Or maybe it was my blood. It was too dark to be sure. I took deep, gasping breaths, trying to stop my head from spinning. The shadow had fled, the screaming within replaced by the screaming of the girls in their cages.

Together, Melanie and I crawled across the floor, dragged ourselves up to reach the locks. We searched through Jessica's pockets until we found the keys and were finally able to unlock them. The five girls scrambled around us, shivering and crying as Melanie and I embraced them.

I searched through Logan's pockets until I found my cell phone. As carefully as my shaking hands would dial, I called the police.

"McGuire," he said, his voice sounding as though I'd woken him.

"It's Richard Harrison," I said, the words harsh and rough, forced through my abused throat.

"It's late. Everything okay?"

"I found them." I looked at the circle of five faces, tears streaking their far-too-young faces. "I found them all."

FORTY-ONE

The Dublin Police Department arrived within minutes. They wanted to take Melanie and me to the hospital, but we insisted on waiting for the detective to arrive from Savannah.

Ambulances came, followed by more cops and paramedics and firemen and still more cops. A constant stream passed by as Melanie and I sat on the bumper of an ambulance holding hands while they attended to our wounds.

I called my parents, but they'd already heard from McGuire and were on their way to Dublin. I winced in pain as a particularly deep cut was bandaged. When he was done, the paramedic patted me on the shoulder and walked off, leaving us alone.

"Why?" Melanie whispered, her head resting on my shoulder.

"Why what?"

"All of it, everything," she said. "My father, Richard. He killed all those girls."

I closed my eyes, leaning my cheek on her hair. There was so much to say; at the same time, there was nothing to say. Words just seemed insignificant, so I squeezed her tighter and pressed a soft kiss into her forehead.

She shivered in my arms and then sniffled, running her hand over her face as she looked at me. Her dark blue eyes glistened with tears. "I'm just like him," she whispered.

"No," I said, but she didn't seem to hear.

"I killed her," she said, her voice lonely and lost. "It wasn't the shadow. It was me."

I shook my head as she cried, but no matter what I said, she didn't seem to hear.

By the time Detective McGuire arrived it was close to midnight, and only then did Melanie stop crying. I told him the story, as much of it as I'd pieced together, Melanie silent next to me.

Before I finished, he was called away and Melanie shivered against me. "Thanks."

"For what?"

"Talking."

"You're welcome."

"You know, I'm not sure where my car is," she said, looking around at all the flashing lights illuminating the farm.

"It's okay. I'll drive."

Detective McGuire returned to us. "Your father wasn't home when the police got there," he said to Melanie. "Any idea where he might be?"

As she shook her head, we heard my parents calling to us from the other side of the crime scene tape. Their words were a babble as they wrapped Melanie and me in their embrace, their strong arms swallowing us. I paid no attention to what they were saying. It was enough to be held.

"Do you want me to drive?" my father asked, still holding me in a hug. "I can take your car and you two can ride with Mom."

I shrugged and backed up to look at him, slightly surprised to notice he was no longer taller than I was. "I couldn't sleep right now if I wanted to," I said. "I think driving might do me good."

With a policeman escorting us, I led Melanie and my parents across the wildflower-strewn fields to the Neon, which started on the first try.

Melanie yawned as she buckled herself in.

I yawned back with a smile. "You okay?" I followed my father's car out of Dublin for the long drive to Savannah.

"No," she said, her voice already thick with sleep. "Maybe? Ask me again in a year. It's just all so—"

"I know."

"She's gone, isn't she?" Melanie asked. "Really gone? I just hope she's happy, wherever she is now."

By the time I thought of a reply, Melanie was asleep, leaving me alone, the shadow nowhere to be found. And, I prayed, finally at peace.

———

It was close to one a.m., almost an hour outside Savannah, when my cell phone rang, waking Melanie.

"Your dad needs gas," my mom said. "We're getting off at the next exit, okay?"

"That's fine."

"How are you doing?"

I turned to Melanie and shook my head. "We're good," I said, not meaning a word of it as I hung up.

As the exit approached, the phone rang again. Max's voice was far too loud out of the phone's tinny speaker.

"Max?" I said. "It's the middle of the night. Is something wrong?"

"Caitlin's missing," he said, his voice on the edge of panic. "They were supposed to stay home, but Sidney wanted ice cream. She promised she'd check in, but that was hours ago. I called the police. I don't know what else to do. I've been driving all over Savannah looking but I can't find them."

"We'll be right there," I said.

The streetlights flashing by cast twisting, writhing, raging shadows across the car, screaming with a desperate fire. And then the shadow came home to Melanie and me with a brilliant, unquenched vengeance.

The Neon hit ninety, ninety-five, leaving my parents behind as we raced toward Savannah. Toward Melanie's father and two more missing girls.

FORTY-TWO

The shadows pressed on my foot, forcing the Neon to cross one hundred miles per hour. The car shivered, the steering wheel alive and fighting against me.

The phone rang once more. Melanie reached for it and put it on speaker.

"Hello?"

"You didn't stop," my mom said.

"We'll meet you at the house, okay?" I said, my knuckles turning white from squeezing the wheel.

"Okay. Just go straight home."

"Where else would I go?"

"Where are we going?" Melanie asked after hanging up with my mother.

"The police already went to your house," I said. "That really only leaves one place."

"You think he'd go to the island?"

My foot trembled, pressing the car to go even faster. One hundred and five. One hundred and ten. South on 95. Past Richmond Hill and off the highway, still breaking the speed limit, following Bryan Neck Road to Fort McAllister and Savage Island. The wooden bar blocking the entrance to the island came into view of the headlights.

"Duck!"

The Neon smashed into the barrier, the windshield absorbing the blow, spiderweb cracks cascading across it. A series of potholes bounced the car as first one and then another tire blew out. Out of control, the car spun in circles in the middle of the empty parking lot until we came to a rest against the guardrail at the edge of the woods.

"Are you okay?" I asked, but Melanie was already scrambling out of the car.

The old deer track had been widened by all the police traffic on it lately, and in the pale moonlight it was easy to follow. Melanie and I raced through the trees, ignoring the cold night air and the bitter wind. The sounds of the island were muted, as though the animals were all asleep, having nightmares of predators let loose among them.

We reached the clearing. The dirt and leaves were all jumbled, filling the air with the scent of freshly dug earth and, beneath it all, a subtle perfume of corruption and decay. In the moonlight, a man rested his bloody palms against the towering oak tree, blood running like sap.

At his feet, two bodies lay unmoving, dark red staining their ripped clothes. Caitlin's long blonde hair was clumped and matted. Pale skin glowed in the faint light, exposed where her clothes didn't cover. Her outstretched hand clutched her sister, and only when I saw the delicate rise and fall of their chests did my own breathing resume.

Melanie choked back a sob. The man looked up at the sound, letting his hands slide down the tree, leaving bloody handprints behind.

"Daddy?"

He turned around and turned around and then there were shadows everywhere. They were a darkness born alive, a living thing bellowing on the edge of hell, thundering with a thousand voices, with Melanie's voice, with my own. A chorus of the damned, of the murdered innocent dead. A whisper, a prayer, a curse.

Scratches dripped blood on his face as he stared at us from wild eyes. For a moment no one moved, and then Melanie and I stepped into the clearing, our shadows almost reaching her father. He knelt and grabbed Caitlin's sister. Sidney moaned in pain but didn't wake as he lifted her, fresh blood pulsing out of a wound in her side.

From his pocket he took out a knife, a flash of silver in the moonlight momentarily breaking through the shadows. "Stay back or she dies." He held the tip beneath Sidney's chin, pushing her head to the sky with the force of it.

When I reached for Melanie, her skin was ice, alive with barely restrained fury like a volcano about to erupt.

"You look just like her," her father said, the words hissed and harsh as he drove the blade farther up until Sidney was staring at the moon. He bent to place a single kiss on the young girl's forehead. "She looks just like you. They all looked just like you."

"I . . ." Melanie said in a cascading multitude of voices. I found the same word echoing out of my own mouth, unable to keep from speaking as the shadow took over my vocal cords.

"I remember . . ."

The shadows crossed the clearing in a heartbeat, blocking out the moonlight as a curtain of blackness fell upon the world.

"I remember you." Melanie and I echoed the words, speaking for the dead as blood dripped from Sidney's throat.

He was so far away. The bare branches of the tree reached to the sky, casting vicious shadows around the clearing. There was no possible way to reach the girl in time as he stabbed the knife deeper into her flesh. I stumbled as I leapt across the clearing, refusing to give up and watch her die.

The shadows screamed.

The shadows burned.

I was too slow to save her, but it didn't matter. The shadows reached him first.

From the darkness, from the threshold of damnation, Melanie's father bellowed a wordless cry.

Smoke poured from his skin like sweat. His eyes glowed like embers sparking off a roaring fire. He screamed. And it was a joyous, blessed, holy prayer. He burned. And it was a glorious, hallowed, sacred fire.

He roared his defiance, his voice rough and harsh, filled with smoke and steam as the blood boiled in his veins. He stumbled through the clearing, flames licking at his skin. He grabbed for Melanie and she stumbled backward, collapsing to the ground in a ball at her father's feet.

"I never should have let you out of your box," he said, his voice a broken growl. He towered above her, casting a blinding shadow against her skin.

The shadows writhed, wrapping themselves around her, and her dark, dark eyes blazed in their embrace. She pushed herself up, fighting against memory and history and the unrelenting heat to stand unbowed in front of her father.

I reached out to her, but she didn't need my help as she stood there watching him burn. He took one lumbering step after another, trying to escape the shadows within, but there was nowhere for him to hide. Nowhere for him to run. His smoking fist lashed out but I jumped in front of her and took the blow, the heat nothing but a distant ache.

Melanie took a step forward and stood beside me, facing her father. "Never again," she said, placing her hands on his chest. Steam surrounded us as she pushed.

He staggered to the ground, his defiant roar fading away. The shadows raged around him as pieces of his flesh fell like sparkling embers.

There was a subtle beauty to the music of the flames, singing a song of apocalypse and salvation and redemption. Moonlight filled the clearing as the shadows disappeared inside him until he was finally gone, nothing but dust and ashes blowing away in the wind off the ocean.

FORTY-THREE

Once more, I called Detective McGuire, and once more, he raced across southern Georgia, arriving on Savage Island as the first rays of the sun peeked above the Atlantic. The paramedics had already taken Caitlin and her sister, promising us they'd take good care of them.

The police wanted to keep us there, asking the same questions again and again, but Detective McGuire stared them down.

"Let them be," he said. "They've earned some rest."

He was silent as he led us to the Neon, Melanie and I holding hands as we had every moment since her father had burned to death. The detective glanced at the broken windshield on my car and just kept walking to his own car, holding the door open for us. On the drive home he stayed quiet as Melanie fell asleep on my shoulder.

When we got there my parents came rushing out of the house, holding Melanie and me in a jumble of arms as the detective drove off. We entered without a word, where they let Melanie crawl into bed with me. My parents stood there after turning the light off, the shadows in the room merely shadows.

"She can stay here as long as she wants," my mom said, glancing over her shoulder at my father.

"In her own room," he said, as they shut the door and left us to sleep.

———————

Some time later, as the setting sun shone brightly through the window, Melanie looked up from where her head rested on my chest.

"I miss her," she said, staring around the room at all the drawings of Melanie Elizabeth Bellemeade, searching the corners, searching for shadows.

"I know," I said, caressing her warm skin, missing the ice of the shadow within her.

"I want to sing." She smiled, but it was little more than a ghost of a smile. "Don't you want to paint?"

"You can sing."

"No," she said, the smile melting into memory. "I want to sing with her."

I pulled her deeper into my embrace, placing a kiss on her shiny, delicate lips. Her arms wrapped around me, the kiss returned for just a moment until a knock on the door broke us apart.

"It's dinner time," my mom said, poking her head in. "If you're hungry."

"No, thanks," I said.

This time, when she left, the door stayed opened.

"I think that's a hint," Melanie said.

"You know," I said, "I think you're right."

She brushed her lips against my cheek. "Now what?"

"The detective called while you were sleeping." I sat up, pulling her with me. "He said they're all going to be okay."

"Thank God," she said.

"He still has lots of questions for us, when we're ready."

"Whenever that is."

"I'm pretty sure he meant tomorrow." I stood and walked to my desk, shuffling through different paintings and drawings and doodles until I had a whole stack of similar pictures, which I shoved into my backpack. I looked at Melanie, where she sat in the fading rays of the sunset pouring through the window. Even having just woken, even after racing through Georgia, even covered in scratches and bandages, she was beautiful. She was alive and here. She was home, and the desperate longing and the bottomless loneliness were complete, and I was finally whole again.

———

I had to borrow my mother's car, since the Neon was broken on the island and Melanie's car was still lost in Dublin somewhere. In perfect silence, I held her hand for the entire drive to Bonaventure.

A blazing sunset cast orange and red fire across the ancient tombstones and statuary, filling the cemetery with color and life as night fell. At the edge of Melanie's grave, moonlit shadows played around us, silent in the chilly autumn air.

"I used to come here all the time," I said, sliding my backpack off. One by one I pulled the drawings out, handing them to Melanie. I shone my flashlight at her mother's tombstone and then at the paintings, showing her the similarities. Showing her the long, delicate, almost skeletal hand clawing out of the ground.

"I think he buried her here." I knelt and rested my fingers on the delicate grass of her mother's grave. "After moving her from the clearing. He must have buried them together, your mom and Melanie. She was always so happy here."

Next to me, a sob broke free, tears slipping from her dark, dark eyes. The moon cast shadows around us, and when I reached for Melanie, her arctic skin was soft and welcoming as I burned with an infinite, undying fire. The shadow of a kiss traced my lips with a whispered cry, and as she smiled I knew, without doubt, without question, without fear, that my best friend was blessedly, gloriously home.

I'd sworn to tell the truth. Melanie's touch was a soft caress shivering through me as I took them both in my arms, wrapped in an endless embrace. The whole truth. Together, always, we screamed so very sweetly while the shadows danced and twirled and sang within one eternal sacred kiss. Nothing but the truth.

So help me God.

Acknowledgments

I owe a tremendous amount of gratitude to a large number of people for help in creating this book. It wouldn't exist at all if not for a conversation with fellow horror author C.W. LaSart (http://www.cwlasart.com) who made me look at the word "ghostly" in a whole new light.

As always, my alpha and beta readers amaze me with their tremendous donation of time and energy to my writing. For this book, my readers were Terri Molina, Ken Salomon, Sue Gravina, Lisa Rashke, Authoress, Lynne Hansen, and Patrick Freivald. Also, while not a beta reader, I wanted to thank Laurie Thompson who was working on her own book at the same time. The mutual support system was a tremendous help.

In addition, I couldn't have made it through this book without the incredible support of my dearly missed writing group back in Chapel Hill (Annette deFerrari, Julie Krantz, Melissa Payne, Ki-Wing Merlin, Julie Fortenberry, Chris Hoerter, Anna Ouchchy, Sue Soltis, and Jeehyun Kim Hoke). I am also fortunate enough to be involved with another amazing group of writers, the MSFV Secret Society. One of those authors, Angela Ackerman, provided a valuable service to the book with her indispensable guide that all writers should have: The Emotion Thesaurus.

Special thanks need to go to my wonderful agency, Erin Murphy Literary; my amazing agent, Ammi-Joan Paquette; and the rest of the Gangos who infuse EMLA with such grace, humor, and talent. This book owes so very much to the continued friendship, support, and Editorial Brilliance of Brian Farrey-Latz. I am humbly indebted to Brian and the rest of the team at Flux, specifically Sandy Sullivan and, always, Lisa Novak, who is the artistic genius behind the fantastic covers for this book and for *Henry Franks*.

For the police matters, I am indebted to Sergeant Josh Mecimore of the Chapel Hill, NC Police Department and Public Information Officer Mike Puetz of the St. Petersburg, FL Police Department. For medical questions, I'd like to thank Lauren Wright of NC Neuropsychiatry.

For teaching me just how much I don't know about music, which is a lot, I owe a tremendous debt to Seth Bisen-Hersh, who read over every single section of the book that dealt with either playing an instrument or singing. Jillian Boehme then helped correct everything I still had wrong.

As always, any mistakes are mine alone.

Finally, despite having lived in Savannah for two years, I would never have been able to paint such a vivid picture of this beautiful jewel of a city without the unending support and assistance of Jon Cohen. Jon not only told me ghost stories about the city that actually appeared in the book, he took countless pictures of any random thing I asked him to take. Then, when it came time for me to choose a high school to set the novel in, his son, Max, started attending Savannah Arts Academy High School.

To thank Max for his assistance, which included answering some of the most random questions I've ever asked, I promised that I wouldn't kill off the character I based on him. I did, however, kill off the character I named after my oldest son.

Which brings me, at last, to my family. I wouldn't be able

to write these stories without the love and dedication of my family. I can't thank my wife, Dr. Anna Salomon, enough, as well as our three wonderful sons, Andre Logan, Joshua Kyle, and Adin Jeremy. Also, thanks to my parents, Robert and Claudia Salomon, for their never-ending encouragement as well as to my sister, Shayna Steinfeld, and her husband, Bruce, and their three sons for all they have always done for me and my family.

I write, as always, for my grandfather, Andre Scara Bialolenki. I'm thanking him again because seeing his name in print is a dream come true. And one of his greatest dreams was to see me published. Now, I know, he's an angel.

About the Author

Peter Adam Salomon is the author of *Henry Franks* (Flux 2012) and of short fiction that has appeared in the *Demonic Visions 50 Horror Tales* series and *Gothic Blue Book III: The Graveyard Edition*. He is a member of the Society of Children's Book Writers and Illustrators, the Horror Writers Association, the International Thriller Writers, and the Authors Guild, and currently lives in St. Petersburg, Florida, with his wife and three sons.

For more information, please visit http://www.allthose brokenangels.com and www.peteradamsalomon.com.